# The School Bully Is My Brother

## By

## Mike Bloemer

First Edition
First Printing 2016

SUMMARY: 13-year old Harold O'Connell joins forces with the biggest bully in school in an all-out attempt to stop their parents' wedding.

Printed in the United States of America

**Hot Flash Entertainment**

**Copyright May 2016**

If you have questions or comments, please email me at
**mikebloemerbooks@gmail.com**

Books by Mike Bloemer


**The School Bully Is My Brother**


**Renegade**


**The Adventures Of Hairball & 'Hot Flash' Granny**


**Adventures Of A Mad Scientist**

Chapter One

The worst day of my life started like any other… horribly.

I was dreaming about being popular, with lots of cool friends and a hot girlfriend, when a blast of freezing cold water drenched my entire head. I tumbled out of bed and shouted, "Anthony, I'm gonna kill you!"

When I wiped the water from my eyes and looked up, I realized it wasn't my rotten five year old brother who blasted me with a super soaker; it was my senile grandmother.

Granny cackled like she usually does when she forgets to take her medication. Granny was pretty big, so her entire body jiggled when she laughed. Her dyed black hair bounced around and her glasses nearly fell off her face.

I wiped my face with my blanket. "What is wrong with you, Granny? Sometimes you act like you're five."

That got Granny to stop laughing. "Oh brother, now you sound like my mother. I'm 62 years old and she still treats me like I'm 16."

Speaking of the Devil, Great Granny barged into my room and snatched the super soaker out of Granny's hands.

Great Granny was 85, but she didn't look a day over 110. She had curly hair that she tried to dye brown, but it always ended up looking purple.

We weren't allowed to say anything about it, though. We were supposed to pretend it was brown.

"Darlene, how many times have I told you to quit shooting people with water guns? You act like you're five!"

"Oh Mother, loosen up," Granny snapped. "You're always so uptight. Penny told me to wake the kids so they wouldn't be late for school, so that's what I did."

While my grannies bickered, my rotten brother Anthony ran in my room and grabbed his super soaker. He then blasted Great Granny in the face.

Great Granny covered her face and shrieked. Anthony laughed and dashed out of my room while Great Granny ran after him.

"I gotta get my cell phone and record this so I can put it on Face Tube," Granny said, wobbling out of my room.

"You're getting YouTube and Facebook confused again," I called after her. "They're two totally separate… ah, forget it."

I hurried into the bathroom to get a shower so I wouldn't miss school. After that I ran downstairs to grab a bite to eat. As with every morning, the kitchen resembled a war zone.

My mom was at the stove trying to be a 'good mother' and cook everyone a homemade breakfast. I kept trying to tell her Cap'n Crunch was a perfectly acceptable breakfast, but she always ignored me. Right now she was trying to cook bacon. (Notice I said *trying*.) Thick, black smoke floated toward the ceiling, setting off the fire alarm. The toast in the toaster was black and smoldering, and our dog Betty Beagle lapped up a puddle of grease on the floor.

I sat down at the kitchen table next to my 12-year old uncle, Jon. Jon flicked spoonfuls of butter at the wall. I yanked the spoon out of his hand. "Knock that off. Granny won't have any butter to eat later when she has her hot flashes."

Jon spun around in his chair. "Don't talk that way to me, young man. I'm your uncle."

"I'm a year older than you, Jon. If anything, I should be telling you what to do."

"That's it, bend over and take off your pants. I'm giving you a whooping."

I groaned and put my head in my hands. Jon was always going on about how I needed to 'respect my elders' whenever I argued with him. While it *was* true he was my uncle (Granny had him one year after I was born), I was actually his elder. But he never listened to me.

I finally got fed up and shoved Jon to the floor. He immediately started crying. Mom ran over and helped him up.

"Harold, knock it off!" she hollered before scurrying back over to the stove.

Granny, Great Granny, and Anthony eventually came into the kitchen. Shortly afterwards Uncle Chucky walked in.

"What's up, everybody?" Chucky asked in the middle of a yawn.

Everyone else grunted. I, on the other hand, smiled and said, "I'm doing great, Chucky. My friends and I finally beat the newest *Call of Honor* game the other day."

Chucky parted the long, black hair hanging over his face and grinned. The dark sunglasses he always wore slid down his nose, revealing his hazel eyes. "Whoa, that's awesome, man. We'll all have to play one day when I get some time."

"Yeah, that'd be cool!" I cleared my throat and said, "Er, I mean, whatever."

I always tried to act cool around Chucky. Even though he was 16 and I was only 13, he never treated me like a little kid. Plus, he always protected me from bullies whenever he saw them picking on me. He was my savior.

I think Chucky liked me because I was one of the few people in the family who didn't freak when he came out two years ago. Half our family eventually came to embrace his 'out-ness', and the other half pretended like he never came out to begin with. Chucky was cool with it, though. He never cared what people thought about him. He did whatever he wanted, another reason I looked up to him.

Chucky picked at the plate of burnt bacon. "Mmm, looks tasty, sis."

Mom kissed Chucky on his head. "Thank you, dear." She then snatched the super soaker away from Anthony, who was blasting poor Betty Beagle in the face. Chucky smirked at me and dropped a couple strips of burnt bacon on the floor, which Betty quickly snatched up.

I glanced at the clock on the wall and hollered, "Holy shnikey, we're gonna miss our bus!"

Jon and I rushed for the door. Before we could run outside, Mom said, "Don't forget, tonight we're all going out for dinner. I want you to meet my new boyfriend. I think he's the one."

Granny snorted orange juice out of her nose. "Ha! You've said that about the last six guys you dated."

"This is different," Mom said, struggling to put out another grease fire.

I couldn't help but roll my eyes. Over the past four years, Mom's dated just about every dude in town. She said she did this so she could find me a 'father figure'.

Jon and I hurried out the door and dashed down the street to the bus stop. It was another mild September morning. The air was cool and sweet, and dew glistened on our neighbor's freshly mowed grass. I envied our neighbor's yard. Our yard was a minefield of dog turds because no one ever picked up after Betty.

Jon and I finally reached the bus stop at the end of the street. My best friend, Abdul, was standing there with his hoodie on, rocking back and forth on his heels.

Abdul had shaggy black hair and a bulging belly, just like me. His parents were Muslims from Pakistan. At home they made Abdul do all sorts of religious stuff. But at school he never talked about his faith, he just acted like a regular kid.

Jon ran over to Abdul and kicked him in his butt. Abdul stumbled forward and flailed his arms. "I told you to stop doing that, idiot!"

Abdul tried to run after Jon, but he was way too slow. Jon cackled and ran around Abdul in circles. He continued to prove my theory that the doctor dropped him on his head when he was born.

My Jewish friend, Blake, was also at the bus stop. We all called him the 'Bionic Man' since he wore glasses, braces, and a hearing aid. Kids liked to turn Blake's hearing aid off because it was funny when he raised his voice when he couldn't hear.

I had just started chatting with Blake when my scrawny Asian friend, Ben, ran over and said, "What's up, Fat-man?"

I narrowed my eyes. "I told you to quit calling me that."

Ben held up his hands. "Hey, I didn't mean to hurt your feelings." He was quiet for a minute, then, to the tune of the old Batman song, sang, *"Na-na-na-na-na-na-na-na Fat-man!"*

I lunged for Ben, but he sprinted to the other side of the street.

It was bad enough that one of my best friends picked on me, but things got even worse when my arch-nemesis walked over. He was a popular, African-American jock by the name of Shawn Farmer. We had been going at it ever since kindergarten when I peed my pants and he pointed it out to the entire class.

Shawn sauntered up to me and said, "Hey fatty."

From the other side of the street, Ben sang, *"Na-na-na-na-na-na-na-na Fat-man!"*

"You ready to get killed during football practice?" Shawn taunted.

"Shut up, Shawn," I mumbled. "I'm not in the mood."

"Awww, what's wrong? Did widdle Harold pee his pants again?"

"I haven't peed my pants since the fifth grade, jerk."

Shawn shook his head and scoffed.

"You are pathetic, O'Connell. I can't wait for my dad to make you run laps later."

I gritted my teeth as Shawn walked over to his friends. Not only was my mortal enemy the most popular kid in school, but his dad was our principal and football coach. Whenever I went to him about his son, he would give me detention for the stupidest reasons, or make me spend our entire football practice running around the field. It got to the point where I was better off just putting up with Shawn's bullying.

I was glad when the bus arrived. No one acted up around our bus driver, Mrs. Spear. She used to be in the military, and she looked like a menopausal female Incredible Hulk.

As soon as the bus skidded to a halt and the door flew open, she bellowed, "Get in here, you little twerps. And I better not hear a peep out of any of you. Mrs. Spear has a throbbing migraine."

We all quietly trudged onto the bus. I sat in the front with Abdul, Ben, and Jon. Shawn and his cronies made their way to the back. I always sat as close to Mrs. Spear as I possibly could. It was the only time during the day when I was safe from buttheads like Shawn.

So like I said before, the beginning of my worst day ever started out pretty bad. But it wasn't too different from any other weekday morning. The really bad stuff started happening after I got to school. (Keep in mind this *still* isn't the worst part.)

Chapter Two

My first class was English with Ms. Hornswaggle. Ms. Hornswaggle was hands down the meanest teacher at William Henry Harrison Middle School. (Yes, our school was named after the president who died after only 30 days in office. Every school in our league was named after a terrible president. It's mostly because all the richer schools in the better leagues took all the good presidents.)

Ms. Hornswaggle was a hefty woman who always wore a muumuu with kittens on it. She also had a black cat named Ms. Meow Meow, who she actually brought to class. Ms. Meow Meow walked up and down the aisles while Ms. Hornswaggle scribbled stuff on the chalkboard. If Ms. Meow Meow caught any kids sleeping, doodling, or cheating, she meowed. Ms. Hornswaggle would then give the 'bad student' a detention. Ms. Meow Meow was like an evil spy.

So anyway, while Ms. Hornswaggle wrote her lesson plan on the board, I looked out the window and daydreamed. I had just started to doze off when a sopping wet spitball splattered against my cheek. I spun around and glared at Shawn, who was sitting up front, holding a straw. I yanked out my own straw and slobbered all over a small ball of paper. I was just about to hurl it at Shawn's head when Ms. Meow Meow rubbed up against my leg. I yelped and accidentally shot the spitball at Ms.

Hornswaggle, just as she turned around and opened her mouth to talk. Let's just say spitballs aren't Ms. Hornswaggle's favorite thing to eat for breakfast. I immediately got a detention.

Art class wasn't much better. I had just finished my clay sculpture of a dragon and was on my way to the drying table when Shawn stuck out his leg. I tripped and reached for the table, hoping to break my fall. That turned out to be a horrible idea, as the table flipped over and dozens of clay sculptures went flying all over the place. Within a matter of seconds, dozens of kids were covered in clay. That got me another detention.

Lunch was even worse. I was chilling with Abdul, Ben, Blake, and our only female friend, Penelope, when Shawn and his cronies tossed food at us. We fired back. But of course I had to overthrow my milk carton, which splattered all over Principal Farmer's new suit. He hollered at me and gave me another detention slip.

Thankfully my teachers were kind of dumb and didn't really talk to each other, so I only had to serve one hour of detention after school. That was the good news. The bad news was, I was late to football practice, which meant Principal Farmer, our head coach, made me run extra laps. After that I had to be on the defensive scout team.

Shawn was our star quarterback, and one of the reasons he was so good was because of our offensive line. The center was a big, bald, ugly dude named Jasper Dunce. His cousins, Rufus and Cletus Dunce, were the guards. Rufus and Cletus (who I liked to call Tweedle Dee and Tweedle Dum) were identical twins.

The Dunces weren't the brightest people on the planet, but they were good football players.

They were so good, in fact, that opposing teams called them the 'Dunce Wall'. But they were also mean turds who always picked on me and my friends. That's probably why they were Shawn's best pals.

I spent the next twenty minutes getting knocked on my butt, as did the rest of the defensive scout team. The only player who managed to slip through the offensive line and tackle Shawn was one of my best pals, Penelope Rodriguez.

Penelope was a big, tough Hispanic girl. She was also the only girl on the football team. It was rumored her grandparents were illegal immigrants, but we weren't allowed to talk about that. She had long, black hair, so kids called her a Mexican Rapunzel.

Coach Bebop, our defensive coach, clapped and shouted, "Way to go, Penelope! Show them boys who's boss!"

Coach Bebop had spiky black hair and always had a whistle dangling from her neck. She was very athletic and health conscious. She could always be seen chomping on carrot sticks or alfalfa sprouts. She was a woman coaching a man's sport, which is why I think she liked Penelope so much. She loved seeing girls beat up guys.

Coach Heffer, our offensive coordinator, put his hands around his mouth and shouted, "BLOCK, OFFENSIVE LINE! BLOCK!"

A bunch of us defensive guys started cracking up. Coach Heffer was a horrible coach. All he ever said was, "Block!" or "Don't let them get the quarterback!" I don't think he knew anything about football. The only reason he got a coaching job was because he and Coach Farmer were childhood friends.

Speaking of Coach Farmer, he paced back and forth on the sidelines, kicking dirt. Coach Farmer looked just like Shawn, except he had a lot less hair, a bigger belly, more wrinkles, and he was white. (Shawn's mom was African-American, which explained his darker skin tone.) Coach Farmer was always stressed, probably because our team was so horrible. We were in the worst league in town, and we had a 1-2 record. Our school hadn't won a league championship since the Eisenhower Administration. (At least, that's what Great Granny said.)

Coach Farmer blew his whistle. "Bring it in, guys!"

We all knelt around Coach Farmer in a giant circle.

Coach Farmer patted Shawn and the Dunces on their heads. "Good job today, guys. You too, Penelope. The rest of you were horrible!"

Abdul grumbled under his breath, "Maybe we would be better players if we had better coaches."

Ben, Blake, and I chuckled. Coach Farmer shot us a dirty look, then whipped out his clipboard and put on his reading glasses.

"As you all know, we're currently 1-2, and we only have three more games left in the season. We gotta win all those games in order to clinch the league championship. If we do that, we go to the playoffs. We play Hoover Middle School this Friday, and with a 0-3 record, they're even worse than we are. Our next two opponents are Buchanan Junior High and Nixon Academy. There's no reason we can't beat them. So let's beat 'em!"

"Um, okay," I said.

Coach Farmer ran his fingers through his

thinning hair and grinned. "Alright gang, I'm ending practice a little early today. I've got a hot date tonight!"

"Dad," Shawn grumbled. "No one wants to hear that."

Coach Farmer patted Shawn on the back. "I think this is the one, son. You might have a new momma sooner than you think."

"DAD!" Shawn shouted.

Coach Farmer and Shawn walked over to their car and drove off. The rest of us had to stay behind and put away all the equipment. After that me, Abdul, Ben, Blake, and Penelope waited out front for my granny to pick us up. About fifteen minutes later, she peeled into the parking lot in her mini-van.

Granny threw open the passenger door. "Hey kids!"

"Hello, Granny," my friends said. They called my granny 'Granny', too, for some weird reason.

Once we buckled up, Granny sped out of the parking lot and cut off a school bus.

"Slow down, Granny," I said, grabbing the dashboard. "You already have 10 points on your license. You don't need anymore."

Granny blew raspberries. "None of those cops knew what they were talking about. Everyone goes 90 on the highway."

"Weren't you in a school zone the last time you got a ticket?" I asked.

Granny turned up the radio to drown me out.

After Granny dropped off my friends, she pulled into our driveway and hopped out of the car. I stumbled out, clutching my stomach. I got carsick whenever I rode with my wacky granny.

I staggered inside our house, nearly tripping over Betty. Betty barked, expecting me to give her a treat.

"I don't have anything, Betty. Besides, you're getting kind of big. Maybe you should lay off the snausages."

Betty said, "Woof," which I guess is dog-speak for, "Look who's talking, tubby."

"Hey Bookie!"

I glanced into the kitchen and groaned. Aunt Patty and Aunt Kathy were sitting at the table. Mom must have invited them for dinner. I loved my aunts, but they were kind of annoying. Especially when they called me 'Bookie'.

Aunt Patty and Aunt Kathy were twin sisters. They were born a few years before my mom. Aunt Patty had black hair and Aunt Kathy had red hair. Other than that, they looked exactly alike. They used to smoke, but after Aunt Kathy had a cancer scare last year, they both decided to quit. Now their arms were covered with nicotine patches. They also drank coffee like it was water, which was why they were so jittery.

Chucky walked into the kitchen with Jon. He nudged me in the side and quietly said, "Uh oh, the house is infested with aunts."

I chuckled. "Where's the Raid when you need it?"

Jon opened the cabinet under the sink and whipped out a can of Raid. "I found it, guys!"

Chucky shouted, "Wait, we were just joking! Don't…"

He was too late. Jon ran up to the aunts and sprayed them with Raid. It only got on their clothes, but they screamed bloody murder anyway.

Granny wobbled into the kitchen and

cackled. "You got them good, Jon! You got them good!"

Mom rushed into the kitchen and snatched the Raid out of Jon's hands. "Mother, this isn't funny! I'm trying to get ready for dinner and you guys are about to make me have a mental breakdown!"

Mom turned to Jon. "Why did you spray the aunts with Raid?

Jon started to cry. He hated being yelled at. Sobbing, he said, "Chucky said the aunts were here, and Harold asked where was the Raid, so I got the Raid and sprayed the aunts."

Jon continued bawling. Mom must have felt bad because she patted him on the head and said, "There there, it's alright."

Once Jon calmed down, Mom turned to me and shouted, "Quit putting bad thoughts in your uncle's head!"

"Are you kidding me?" I said. "Jon is barely a year younger than I am. You act like he's five."

Mom gave Jon a hug. "You know my little brother is… special."

Chucky, Granny, and I covered our mouths so Mom wouldn't hear us laugh.

Jon turned to me and grinned. "Did you hear that? Penny says I'm special."

This time Chucky, Granny, and I burst out laughing.

"That's it, go upstairs and get ready!" Mom exploded. "You too, Mother!"

The three of us ran upstairs (well, Granny wobbled) and got dressed.

Mom wanted us to dress halfway decent because we were going to Uncle Bob's All-You-Can-Eat Buffet. Uncle Bob's wasn't really that fancy of a restaurant (they had a sign that said 'No shoes, no shirt, no problem!'), but it was the nicest restaurant we could afford. My family really didn't have that much money. My grannies didn't get a lot from social security, and Mom had to work long hours at Simo's Diner just to make ends meet. Our 'big nights out' usually involved going to McDonalds and splurging off the dollar menu.

I threw on a flannel shirt and jeans, the nicest outfit I had, and thundered downstairs. I had just walked by the front door when the doorbell rang.

"Can you get that, dear?" Mom hollered from the kitchen, where my aunts were still wiping Raid off their pants. "Jon dropped milk all over the floor."

I rolled my eyes. Of course he did.

I opened the door and said, "Come on in. We'll be ready to go in…"

My jaw nearly dropped to the floor. Standing on the front porch were Shawn and Coach Farmer.

Shawn cocked an eyebrow and stepped back. "O'Connell? Wha…"

He turned to Coach Farmer, who looked just as shocked as I was.

"I think we have the wrong place, Dad."

Coach pulled out a piece of paper and studied the house number on our mailbox.

"I don't think so. This looks like the same house I dropped her off at last week."

I shook my head. "Wait a minute, dropped who off?"

Coach Farmer scratched his thinning head. "My girlfriend."

My heart started beating like crazy. Coach

Farmer had been talking about how he had a hot date. Could he… no, that was impossible.

Shawn must have started to think the same thing because his dark face turned ghostly pale.

"No…" he muttered, stumbling backwards.

Coach looked at us like we were nuts. He obviously hadn't figured it out yet (no surprise there).

Mom walked over as she stuck a loop earring in her ear.

"Is that Sam, Harold? Let him in."

I turned to Mom and said, "So wait, this is… you're going out with…"

Mom grabbed my shoulders. "Are you okay, dear? You look sick."

I gulped down the bile rising up my throat. "I think I'm about to be."

Mom stepped outside and gushed, "Oh Sam, don't you look handsome."

Coach blushed and giggled like a little kid. He still wore the same tucked in golf shirt and khaki shorts he had on during practice. Mom apparently had low standards.

Mom looked at Shawn and smiled. "Sam, is this your son? He is so adorable!"

I clutched my stomach and puffed out my cheeks. I was about to hurl chunks.

Even though it was obvious what was going on, I still held out hope it was all a big misunderstanding. Maybe Coach was just dropping something off. Maybe he wanted to talk about my detention.

But then Mom did something to dash all those theories. She threw her arms around Coach Farmer's neck and kissed him on the lips.

"Ewww!" Shawn and I blurted out at the

same time.

The rest of my family came outside.

"Let's go!" Great Granny hollered. "We're gonna miss the senior early bird special!"

As we made our way to Granny's giant mini-van, Shawn brushed up against me and whispered, "Don't mention any of this at school. My reputation will be ruined if anyone finds out I went to dinner with your family."

"Hey, I'm not too happy about it, either," I grumbled. "We have to make sure this is our parents' last date."

Shawn cracked a smile. "You read my mind."

With that, Shawn and I hopped into the back of the van. For at least one night, my mortal enemy and I were on the same team.

Chapter Three

"Food fight!"

Granny picked up a buttered roll and tossed it at Great Granny's face.

"Sit down and shut up, Darlene!" Great Granny snapped. "Don't embarrass me in public."

Granny grumbled under her breath, but she did sit down. I'm sure she didn't want her 85-year old mother spanking her behind like she did last week at the grocery store.

Everyone else was busy piling food in their mouths. Since Uncle Bob's was an all-you-can-eat buffet, everyone's plate was covered with spaghetti, chicken, ribs, fish, hamburgers, hot dogs, you name it. Coach Farmer had two plates of food. He kept shoveling grub down his throat like he was never going to eat again. Jon pressed his entire face into his plate of mashed potatoes and ate like a pig. Chucky laughed and encouraged him. Aunt Patty and Aunt Kathy were light eaters, so they nibbled on chicken fingers. Mom patted Coach Farmer on his back to make sure he didn't choke. And Anthony ran around the restaurant with his pants on his head. People at nearby tables gave us dirty looks for being so loud and messy, but I was the only one who noticed.

I glanced at Shawn, who sat across from me. He seemed as miserable as I was.

"So tell me, Sissy, how did you and Sam meet?" Aunt Kathy asked. "Don't be bashful, give us all the dirty details, hehehe."

"Yeah Sissy, we ain't never heard the whole

story," Aunt Patty said.

Mom giggled and grabbed Coach Farmer's hand. "Well, Sam and I met four months ago at the grocery store. We both reached for the same jar of peanut butter. Sam told me I could have it, peanut butter gave him gas anyway, and it was then that I realized he was the one."

I nearly choked on my hotdog.

"What? Are you serious? That's why you guys started dating? That's so stupid!"

"I agree with Harold," Shawn said. "That's a pretty dumb story."

That was the first, and probably *only*, time we'd ever agree with one another.

"I think it's a sweet story, Sissy," Aunt Kathy gushed.

"Thanks, Sissy," Mom said.

"Do your mom and aunts always call each other 'Sissy'?" Shawn whispered.

I smirked. "Yeah, it's pretty dumb, huh?"

"Yeah it is," Shawn chuckled.

We both suddenly stopped smiling. As mortal enemies we weren't supposed to be having fun together. We'd have to be more careful in the future.

"So you really didn't know Sam was Harold's principal and football coach, Sissy?" Aunt Kathy asked, sipping her coffee.

"Yes, and I'm completely embarrassed," Mom said, blushing. "I haven't been able to go to any of Harold's games or conferences because I work so much."

Mom put her hand over her mouth. "I'm a terrible mother."

Coach Farmer wiped barbeque sauce off his face and said, "No you're not, dear. In fact, you're a wonderful mother."

Coach Farmer turned to me and narrowed his eyes. "Isn't that right, Harold?"

I gave Coach a funny look. Usually he called me by my last name. I guess he was pretending to be nice around my mom.

"Yes, Mom is a good mom," I said.

Shawn smirked again. If we didn't watch it, we might just accidentally get along.

A loud oinking sound nearly caused me to fall out of my chair. I spun around and grinned. The owner of Uncle Bob's All-You-Can-Eat-Buffet, Uncle Bob himself, was walking around with his pet pig mascot, Oinky. Oinky had a red leash around his neck, just like a dog would. All the kids in the restaurant squealed and ran over to pet Oinky.

"Oh dear, that doesn't look sanitary," Aunt Kathy mumbled.

Granny handed Great Granny her cell phone. "Take a picture of me with the pig."

Granny got on the floor and hugged Oinky.

Great Granny held up the phone with two fingers, like it was a stinky diaper. "I don't know how to use this thing!"

"I'll take a picture," Chucky said. He whipped out his phone and flashed away while Granny kissed Oinky on the lips.

"Oh Mom, that's nasty," Aunt Patty said.

Much to my surprise, Shawn burst out laughing.

I cocked an eyebrow. "Something funny?"

"Yeah, your goofy family," Shawn chuckled.

"Hey, my family may be a little wacky, but they're not----"

"Calm down, O'Connell," Shawn said,

cutting me off. "I wasn't making fun of them. I'm actually having fun."

This time I raised both eyebrows. "Really?"

"Yeah," Shawn said, sipping his pop. "Most of the time it's just me and my dad. Dinner is usually boring. This is probably the most fun I've had out to eat in a long time."

I really didn't want to feel sorry for Shawn since he had been a jerk to me all my life. But I couldn't help it. I knew what it felt like to lose a parent. I knew he probably missed his mom as much as I missed my dad. But at least I had a bunch of other family members to look out for me. Yeah, they may have gotten on my nerves from time to time (okay, most of the time), but they all had my back. Shawn just had his dad. He was the most popular guy at school, but at home he was all alone.

I was about to say something when Oinky starting squealing.

"I can't hold him much longer," Granny hollered, squeezing Oinky to her chest. "Hurry up and take a few more pictures so I can put them on my TubeFace page."

Shawn nearly spit out his pop. "TubeFace?"

"Don't ask," I said.

Oinky suddenly slipped out of Granny's arms and dashed around the restaurant.

"Stop that pig!" Uncle Bob hollered, jumping to his feet. His bulging belly swung back and forth in his overalls. "He's dangerous when he's not on his leash! He's---"

CRASH!

Oinky had just knocked over a table full of food, splattering it all over the floor. Lumps of mashed potatoes and clumps of spaghetti flew into the air and landed on Aunt Patty and Aunt Kathy.

They both screamed and ran to the bathroom.

Shawn burst out laughing again. Tears streamed down his cheek.

"I'm glad you're enjoying yourself," I said.

Shawn wiped away his tears. "This is the funnest dinner I've had in years."

I shrugged. "This is a pretty normal night for me."

Oinky knocked over a few more tables. Anthony thought it was a game and yanked on tablecloths, spilling even more food on the floor. Customers screamed and ran for the exits. The only people who stayed were Shawn, Coach Farmer, and my family.

Uncle Bob fell to his knees. "My beautiful restaurant! It's ruined! Ruined!"

Mom glanced at her watch and yawned. "Wow, it's getting late. I have to get up early tomorrow. Perhaps we should…"

Mom turned to Coach Farmer and gasped. I gasped, too. And for good reason. Coach Farmer was on his knees, holding up a small ring.

"No," I whispered.

"No," Shawn said, a bit louder.

Granny grabbed Great Granny's arm. "Look, Mother. Sam is proposing."

"I'm not blind," Great Granny snapped.

The aunts returned from the bathroom and squealed like little girls.

"Look Sissy, Sam is asking Sissy to marry him," Aunt Kathy said.

"I know, Sissy, Sissy is gonna need us to help plan the wedding," Aunt Patty replied.

Coach cleared his throat. "Penny, I've loved you since the moment you tried to steal my peanut butter. I know it's only been four months, but I know enough about you to realize I want to spend the rest of my life with you. Penny… will you marry me?"

Before Mom could say a word, I shouted, "Don't do it!"

Mom stared at me in surprise. "What do you mean, dear?"

I threw up my hands. "You just met the guy four months ago. You don't even know him!"

"I know he's a good man," Mom said. "And I know he's a good principal and a good coach. I thought you liked him."

"Are you kidding me? He's a horrible principal, and an even worse coach. You would know that if you were ever home. I complain about him all the time!"

"He does," Granny said, tearing into a chicken leg. "I gotta listen to him all day long."

I looked around at my family. "Doesn't anyone else think this is crazy?"

"I do," Shawn said.

"You do?" I asked. I still wasn't used to Shawn agreeing with me about anything.

He leaned toward me and whispered, "Yeah, do you have any idea what kids at school will say to me when they hear my dad is marrying your mom?"

Shawn turned back to Coach Farmer. "Seriously Dad, you don't know anything about Ms. O'Connell."

"I know that I love her," Coach Farmer replied gruffly.

"And I love you." Mom grabbed the ring and slipped it around her finger.

With tears streaking down her cheeks, Mom said, "I will marry you, Sam. I will."

Coach grabbed Mom's face and gave her a big, wet, sloppy kiss on her lips.

"Get a room, whippersnappers," Great Granny hollered.

While the rest of my family cheered, Shawn and I stared at each other in horror. I knew we were thinking the same thing. Our parents' engagement had to be stopped.

If it wasn't, the school bully would become my brother. Talk about an existential threat!

Chapter Four

I kicked open the front door so hard that it banged against the wall, rattling a bunch of pictures. Betty Beagle jumped off the couch and ran under the table.

"I can't believe you would do this to me, Mom," I cried, storming into the kitchen. "It's bad enough I have to put up with bullies at school. The last thing I need is to have one as a brother!"

"This isn't about you, Harold," Mom shouted. She was on the verge of tears. "Don't I deserve a little happiness?"

The rest of our family quietly walked in after us. Mom and I had argued the entire drive home, and I think it made everyone uncomfortable. Well, everyone but Granny, who always seemed to enjoy people yelling at each other. That was probably why she filled up our DVR list with Jerry Springer and trashy MTV reality shows.

Mom and I continued our shouting match. Jon started to cry, so Chucky took him up to his room. Granny grabbed Anthony, who still had his pants on his head, and took him up to bed, too. Aunt Kathy and Aunt Patty went home, and Great Granny took Betty out. Soon it was just me and Mom.

"Why can't you be happy for me?" Mom said in between sniffles.

I hardly ever cried, but I found myself blinking back tears. "You don't understand, Mom. I can't stand Shawn. He's a jerk. Coach Farmer is just as bad. They make my life at school miserable. And now they're about to ruin my home life. Knowing my luck, they'll move in and I'll have to share a room with Shawn."

I was joking when I said that. But then Mom bit her lip and looked down.

"Mom, are you serious?!" I cried.

Mom threw up her hands. "We're all hard on money, Harold. Sam struggles just like we do. I figured if he and Shawn moved in, we could all save a little."

"I don't believe this," I grumbled. "I need a drink."

I grabbed the milk out of the fridge and drank straight from the carton.

"Oh for Pete's sake, use a glass," Mom said. "You're just as bad as your grandmother."

I stuck out my tongue. "Ew, I think I swallowed one of her whiskers."

I thrust the milk back into the fridge and slammed the door.

Great Granny came back inside with Betty, who danced around in circles and barked. She always did that after going potty because she expected a treat. Great Granny tossed her a milkbone. She then walked past us toward the stairs, holding up her wrinkled, gnarled hand.

"I don't want to get in the middle of this. I think you're all crazy. I wish you'd put me in a home."

Great Granny scurried upstairs before we could respond.

For the first time since Coach Farmer showed up on our front porch, Mom and I smiled at each other.

"I'm going to miss that old bat when she's gone," Mom said.

"Are you kidding me?" I said. "Great Granny is going to outlive us all."

Mom snorted like a pig. She had the goofiest laugh. That, of course, made me laugh. Pretty soon we were both cracking up. Granny came in to the kitchen to grab a bag of Oreos, which she ate every night in bed as she watched Netflix.

"You both are clinically insane," Granny said before grabbing the carton of milk with her whiskers and wobbling upstairs.

Mom wiped away her tears and sighed. "Oh Harold, I don't want us to fight. How about we talk about this tomorrow?"

"Okay," I said, covering up a yawn. "I just have one question. Why is the wedding so soon? I mean, don't most weddings happen a year after the engagement?"

Mom twiddled her fingers, like she was embarrassed about something. She finally said, "Well, as you know, neither of us has a lot of money. And Sam's brother was supposed to get married in three weeks at that nice church down the street. Unfortunately for Sam's brother, his fiancé ran off with another man. But that turned out to be a blessing in disguise, because Sam's brother is letting us use the church. Since he already paid for the wedding and all the refreshments, he figured it might as well go to good use."

Only my family would cash in on a cancelled wedding.

I tried to bite my tongue, but I couldn't help it. "I don't think Dad would want you to do this," I blurted out.

Mom turned pale. She always got upset

when we mentioned Dad.

Mom clutched the kitchen counter. "Your father would want us to be happy."

That just made me angry. "You marrying Coach Farmer doesn't make me happy."

Mom was now clutching the counter so hard, her knuckles had turned white. "I thought we were going to discuss this tomorrow."

"No, you need to call Coach and break the whole thing off *tonight*. It's too soon."

Mom started to cry again. "Mike... your father... has been gone for four years."

"That's not long enough. I don't understand why you're rushing this."

"You need a father figure in your life," Mom said, trying to change the subject. "It'll be good for---"

"Coach Farmer isn't a father figure!" I interrupted. "He's nothing like my father!"

Mom tried to remain calm, which only made me angrier. "Harold, I---"

"I'm sorry I can't get over Dad's death as quickly as you can," I said, unable to stop myself.

Mom's jaw dropped. Rivers of tears streamed down her cheeks.

"Oh Harold, how could you?"

Mom twirled around and ran up to her room.

I immediately felt bad about what I said, but I was just being honest. Ever since Dad died, Mom did everything she could to forget about him. She never mentioned him, she hid all his pictures, and she started seeing other people. It was like the very thought of him caused her to break down. Everyone tip-toed around the topic.

When Mom wasn't around, my family talked about Dad all the time. How couldn't we? He was the most amazing guy any of us had ever known. But around Mom we had to watch what we said. We had to treat her like a 'fragile doll', as Granny liked to say.

I ran up to my room and buried my head in my pillow. I fell asleep in a puddle of tears.

Chapter Five

I had just started to doze off in Ms. Hornswaggle's class when something sharp jabbed me in the cheek. I jumped up and shouted, "I'm awake!"

All my classmates stared at me.

"Smooth, Fat-man," Ben snickered.

Ms. Hornswaggle had been writing our lesson plan on the chalkboard when I screamed. She turned around and snarled while wiping chalk off her kitty cat muumuu. Ms. Meow Meow sauntered up to me and hissed.

"Sleeping in class again, Mr. O'Connell?" she asked icily.

"No, I was just... uh... resting my eyes?"

"DETENTION!" she shrieked.

I groaned and slouched in my seat. Everyone turned back around and watched Ms. Hornswaggle scribble some nonsense about how *Moby Dick* was one of the greatest books ever. Whatever. Everyone knows *Green Eggs & Ham* is the best book of all time. I did a book report on it every year until the third grade, when my teacher gave me an F and said I needed to read 'big boy' books. So I upgraded to the Berenstain Bears.

I was just about to doze off again when I noticed Shawn staring at me.

I gave Shawn a dirty look and mouthed, *"What do you want, bonehead?"*

Shawn pointed at my feet and mouthed, *"Read the note, doofus."*

I glanced down. Sure enough, a balled up piece of paper lay next to my left foot. So that was what woke me up.

I grabbed the ball of paper and flattened it against my desk. The writing was barely legible. It read simply *Meet me in the boiler room after gym.*

I looked up and cocked an eyebrow. *"Why?"*

Shawn was about to say something, but Ms. Hornswoggle shrieked, "Pay attention, Mr. Farmer! Don't make me send you to your father's office!"

Shawn rolled his eyes and turned around. We probably wouldn't get a chance to talk all day (if people saw us together, it would raise more than a few eyebrows), so I'd just have to meet him in the boiler room. Part of me really didn't want to, though. One, I couldn't stand Shawn, and two, how did I know it wasn't a trap? It could be an ambush, so he and the Dunces could pound me in private. But I knew I'd probably go anyway. Maybe he had some good news about our parents' engagement, like that it was called off.

The rest of the day was pretty lousy. I got yelled at in math class for not paying attention, everyone was still mad at me in art class for destroying all the clay sculptures, and for lunch we had vegetable lasagna. Vegetable lasagna! What sort of sick joke was that?

My friends tried to cheer me up, probably because they sensed I was upset. Abdul showed me his new comic book, Ben was nice and called me Husky-Man instead of Fat-Man, and Penelope kept turning Blake's hearing aid on and off. It was hilarious hearing Blake's voice get louder every time she did that.

Still, I couldn't stop thinking about my fight with Mom. I felt horrible about making her cry, but I felt even worse when I thought about how Dad would feel if he knew Mom was trying to replace him with a total loser.

I really wanted my friends' advice, but I couldn't tell them about the wedding. None of them could keep a secret. If word got out about me and Shawn becoming brothers, everyone would talk about it. I didn't mind getting picked on every now and then, but I hated when people gossiped about me.

After lunch we headed to gym. The Dunces swatted me and my friends with towels as we changed. For the first time ever, though, Shawn didn't join in. He even told the Dunces to knock it off. We were all stunned, especially the Dunces.

After we changed, we went upstairs and sat on the gymnasium floor. I grinned as the hottest girl in school, April Summers, plopped down a few rows over from me.

April bounced up and down on the floor as she combed her long, red hair. She had more energy than anyone I knew. She was also super smart. She was my dream girl.

I kept staring at April until she looked directly at me and cocked an eyebrow. I gulped and turned away.

Our gym teachers were Coach Bebop and Coach Heffer. They were standing in the front of the gym, talking about what we should do for the day.

Coach Bebop finally blew her whistle. Everyone in the gym stopped talking.

"Okay kids, let's head out to the softball field. We're playing ball."

As soon as I walked outside, I was blinded by the sunshine and smothered by the heat. It was nowhere near as cool as it was earlier that morning.

"Can't we exercise in the gym, with the air conditioner?" I whined

Coach Bebop blew her whistle in my ear. "No! A little fresh air won't kill you!"

We all jogged over to the softball field. Shawn and all his jock friends were on one team. Me, Penelope, and the rest of our un-athletic pals were on the other team.

Shawn's team was up to bat first, so my team covered all the bases and the outfield. I was on second base, and Penelope pitched.

Penelope was a beast at most sports, but she was a monster when it came to softball. Rufus was the first up to bat, and he actually looked frightened.

"D... don't throw it t...too hard, please," Rufus stammered.

Penelope responded by throwing a 100mph fastball (at least, that was how fast it looked to me). Rufus dropped his bat and covered his head.

"Strike one!" Coach Bebop shouted gleefully.

Penelope threw two more strikes in rapid-fire succession. Rufus trudged over to the sidelines. Jasper and Cletus made fun of him.

Next up was April. Penelope was a pretty good pitcher, but April was an even better batter. She easily hit Penelope's curveball and sent it flying toward second base. I did what I usually did when something flew towards me: I dropped to the ground. The ball walloped Coach Heffer upside the back of his head, knocking him over. (He was standing out on the field, making sure we didn't cheat.) I jumped up just as April passed first base and raced toward me.

"Get the ball, Harold!" Penelope screamed.

I ran over to Heffer, grabbed the ball, and dashed back to base a split-second after April slid over it. A cloud of dust billowed into the air, causing me to choke.

April jumped to her feet and wiped dust off of her shorts. Without looking up, she mumbled, "Sorry if I got you dirty. I'm just really competitive."

I giggled like a love-struck idiot. "Don't worry about it. You're an amazing softball player."

April looked up and smiled. Even more shockingly, she actually looked into my eyes! They were bright blue and a little sparkly. I was in love.

"Thanks," she beamed.

I finally figured out how to get April to like me. I just had to suck up to her.

"Throw the freaking ball, Harold!"

I spun around to find Penelope growling at me. I quickly tossed her the ball.

"Penelope seems angry," April observed. "I wonder what's up her butt?"

I shrugged. "I'm not sure."

While Penelope continued hurling softballs at Cletus' head, I tried to have a little small-talk with the love of my life.

"So… you look good in those shorts."

April narrowed her eyes. They were no longer sparkly. "What did you say, you chauvinist pig?"

April was in all the smart classes and always used big words. I, on the other hand, was in all the dumb classes and had no clue what 'chauvinist' meant. But she also called me a pig, so I'm sure it wasn't a compliment.

If I was smart I would have kept quiet. But I wasn't smart, so I said, "You have great legs."

"Do those lame pickup lines usually work for you?" April asked icily.

"Sadly no," I grumbled.

Cletus finally hit the ball. April mumbled, "Thank God," and took off for third base. I slouched my head and kicked the dirt. I had one chance to woo the hottest girl in school and I totally blew it. My love life was over before it even began.

I noticed Shawn staring at me. I stuck out my tongue. Shawn turned away.

We continued playing for about an hour. Coach Bebop eventually blew her whistle and hollered, "Alright gang, head inside and get changed."

"About time," I grumbled. Even with Penelope as our pitcher, we were getting slaughtered. I lost count how many homeruns Shawn's team hit.

We all filed past Coach Heffer, who was still sprawled out on the ground. Even Coach Bebop ignored him. The guy really wasn't liked at all.

I didn't see Shawn in the locker room. For the first time ever that was a bad thing, because now the Dunces had no one to control them. Thankfully they focused all their bullying on Abdul and Blake, which allowed me to slip out unnoticed. I walked down the hall to the boiler room, opened the door, and stepped inside.

The room was dark except for a single cracked light bulb dangling from the ceiling. Water dripped from a pipe in the back. Something brushed up against my leg. Rumor had it there were mice in the school, so that kind of freaked me out.

I was about to leave when someone grabbed my arm. I screamed bloody murder and slapped my attacker in the face.

"OUCH! Knock it off, bonehead! It's me, Shawn!"

Shawn stepped under the cracked bulb.

"Scare me half to death why don't ya?" I grumbled. "So what do you want? Why are we here?"

Shawn thrust his hand in my face. I flinched, thinking he was about to hit me. When I opened my eyes, I saw that his hand was open.

"I propose a truce."

"A truce?" I repeated. "What do you mean?"

"You and I haven't exactly gotten along over the years," Shawn started to say.

"Oh really?" I interrupted. "I hadn't noticed."

Shawn frowned, but he didn't say anything smart.

"Like I was saying, we haven't gotten along. But we need to put all that behind us, because right now we have a bigger problem."

I nodded. "Right. If our parents get married, our lives are over."

"Exactly. You don't want me and my dad living with you, and I definitely can't have the biggest geek in school becoming my new step-brother. Your geekiness will rub off on me, ruining my social life."

"Hey," I said defensively. "I'm not the biggest geek in school. What about Abdul? Or Ben and Blake?"

"You do have some serious competition," Shawn admitted.

"Okay, I'm with you so far," I said uneasily. "What should we do?"

Shawn nervously glanced around the room out of the corner of his eyes, like he was afraid someone would walk in on us.

"The way I see it, the wedding is in three weeks, so we have three chances to stop it."

"Why only three chances?" I asked.

"Well, with school, football, homework, and all the other stuff we do throughout the week, the only time we'll have a chance to ruin the wedding is on the weekends. And we have three weekends, so that's three chances."

I nodded again. "Okay, so what should we do first?"

"The easiest way to get our parents to break up is to find them better dates," Shawn explained. "So I was thinking we could create two accounts on a dating website, pretend to be our parents, and find people who are young and good-looking. Then we can convince our parents to take us to dinner Saturday night, tell their 'secret dates' to meet us there, and with any luck our parents will fall in love with them."

I stared at Shawn in stunned silence. His plan was insane. But since I couldn't come up with anything better, I said, "That's crazy enough it just might work."

I shook Shawn's hand, catching him by surprise.

"I agree to your truce."

Shawn breathed a sigh of relief. "Cool. It's only a temporary truce, of course. And we can't let anyone suspect anything. I'll have to keep on being mean to you in public."

I shrugged. "Okay. But if you can try and

lay off a bit, like you did today in the locker room, that would be great."

Shawn replied, "I'll see what I can----"

The door suddenly swung open. Standing out in the hall were the three Dunces.

Jasper stepped inside. "There you are, Shawn. We was wondering where you…"

Jasper and his cousins stopped dead in their tracks and stared at us in horror. At first I didn't know why, but then I glanced down.

Shawn and I were still holding hands.

## Chapter Six

Jasper scrunched up his face, as if he smelled a fart.

"Why are you guys holding hands? Are you going on a date or something?"

It was the sort of thing you'd say around your friends to get them to laugh. The only difference was, I wasn't their friends, and no one laughed.

Shawn and I yanked our hands apart. I glanced at Shawn. At first he looked horrified, but he quickly regained his composure.

Shawn walked up to the Dunces and casually said, "What? Don't be stupid. I saw Harold sneak in here, so I… uh…"

Cletus scratched his bald head and said, "I think I figured it out."

"I bet that's a first," I mumbled.

Shawn smirked, but he quickly turned away so the Dunces didn't see him.

"What did you figure out, Cletus?" Jasper asked. "Come on, you can tell us."

It took everything I had not to laugh. Jasper was talking to Cletus like he was three.

Cletus continued scratching his head. "Duh, Shawn must've seen Harold sneak into the boiler room, so he followed him so he could pound his face in."

Rufus and Jasper nodded as if Cletus said the most brilliant thing they ever heard.

Shawn cleared his throat. "Er, yeah, Cletus is right. I was just about to pound Harold's face in, but you guys interrupted me."

"Well, now we can help you," Jasper said, cracking his knuckles.

I closed my eyes and covered my face.

"No!" Shawn suddenly shouted.

I peeked through my fingers. The Dunces stared at Shawn like he lost his mind.

"I mean, I'll handle this." Shawn grabbed my arm and whispered, "Sell this for all it's worth."

Shawn pulled back his fist and punched my arm. There was a loud smacking sound, but the punch didn't hurt. In fact, I barely felt a thing. That was when I realized Shawn used his other arm, the one hidden from the Dunces, to slap his leg.

I quickly put two and two together. "Ouch! That freakin' hurt! You're a jerk!"

The Dunces cackled like sadistic madmen.

Cletus clapped like a baby. "Again! Again!"

Shawn pretended to punch my stomach. I fell to my knees and wailed, "Arrgh! You broke my spleen!"

I fell to the ground, moaning in agony.

Cletus gasped. "Oh no, I don't know what a spleen is, but I think O'Connell's really hurt!"

"Why'd you hit him so hard, Shawn?" Rufus wailed. "If my brother and I get busted for fighting one more time, we gotta go back to juvie!"

"Whoa, calm down, guys," Shawn said. "I didn't hit Harold *that* hard."

I should have quit while I was ahead, but I couldn't help myself. I loved seeing the Dunces so upset. I groaned even louder and mumbled, "I think I'm dying."

Rufus and Cletus started crying. Jasper just

stared at me.

"Someone call 911!" Cletus wailed. "I would, but I don't remember the number!"

Rufus slapped his dim-witted brother upside the back of his head. "No, idiot! If we do that, we'll get arrested for sure! Let's leave his body for the janitor to find!"

Rufus and Cletus dashed out of the boiler room, sobbing uncontrollably.

Jasper continued staring at me. "You seem pretty hurt there, O'Connell."

"I am," I grunted. "Shawn beat the tar out of me. You saw."

Something told me Jasper didn't believe our little act. I couldn't say I was surprised. Jasper wasn't quite as dumb as his cousins. But of course that was like saying a tortoise wasn't quite as slow as a snail. It was true, but they were both pretty dang slow.

Shawn said, "Yeah, well, I've been working out. You know, working on my throwing arm. That's probably why O'Connell is in so much pain."

Jasper nodded, but he still didn't seem convinced.

Shawn whipped out his cell phone. "Gee, look at the time. Practice is about to begin. We better hurry up. You know how much my dad hates it when we're late."

Jasper nodded again. "Yeah, we should probably go. But what are we gonna do about O'Connell?"

"W... what do you mean?" Shawn stammered.

"How do we know he won't rat us out?" Jasper growled.

Shawn glanced at me. "Uh…"

"I won't say a word," I groaned, still pretending to be hurt.

"See?" Shawn said. "He won't say anything. Because if he does…"

Shawn punched his left palm.

I covered my eyes. When I finally peeked through my fingers, Shawn and Jasper were gone. I breathed a sigh of relief. Jasper fell for my horrible acting job. I think.

I stood up and stretched. I still couldn't believe Shawn only pretended to hit me. I could totally get used to that.

I went up to Ms. Hornswaggle's room to serve my detention. I was shocked when Ms. Hornswaggle said Principal Farmer waived it. She didn't seem too happy about it, but she had to do what the principal said. He was her boss!

I dashed back down to the locker room, changed into my gear, and headed out to the practice field. The team gathered around Coach Farmer while he told us what we would be doing that afternoon. As usual, Coach Bebop stood off to the side, chomping on carrots. Coach Heffer gorged on a double-decker sandwich.

I took up my usual spot on the defensive scout team. Jasper lined up directly across from me. He bared his teeth and growled.

I gulped and started shaking. As soon as the whistle was blown, Jasper hiked the ball to Shawn and slammed me to the ground. I groaned as pain shot up my spine.

Jasper hovered over me. "There's plenty more where that came from, punk."

Coach Farmer bopped Jasper upside the back of his helmet with his clipboard. "What are you doing, Dunce? Get back on the line!"

Farmer grabbed my hand and yanked me to my feet. "You okay, son?"

"Yeah, just got the wind knocked out of me," I mumbled.

"Why don't you sit out the rest of the drills?" Farmer suggested. "And how about we not mention this to your mother? She told me to make sure you don't get hurt."

I glanced around the field. Everyone was looking at me funny, including my friends. If Farmer didn't stop treating me so nice, people would grow suspicious. For the first time ever I actually *wanted* him to be mean to me.

Shawn must have sensed things were spiraling out of control because he said, "Whew, I'm hot. How about we take a water break?"

"Good idea, son," Coach Farmer said, "Everyone go wet your whiskers!"

I joined my friends as we made our way over to the water jugs. I grabbed a water bottle and was about to take a sip when Jasper snatched it out of my hand.

"You had a pretty good practice for someone with a ruptured spleen," he sneered.

I felt my face turn pale. How could I have been so stupid? I was supposed to pretend I was still hurt, and like a dunce I completely forgot.

Cletus and Rufus scratched their heads. Since they weren't as bright as their dim-witted cousin, it took them a bit longer to figure things out. The flickering light bulbs hovering over their heads finally stayed on long enough for them to realize I had been playing opossum.

"So O'Connell really wasn't hurt?" Rufus asked stupidly.

Jasper sighed. I guess even he had his limits when it came to his cousins and their ongoing battle with intelligence. "Yes Rufus, he was faking."

"I don't think Harold... er, I mean, O'Connell, was faking it," Shawn said nervously. He nudged me in the side. "Right, O'Connell?"

I clutched my belly. "Uh, yeah... ohhhhhh, my spleen."

Shawn suddenly gasped and muttered, "No...."

At first I didn't know why. But then I saw her.

Mom.

She was walking up the hill, carrying a plastic container. Her long hair was pulled up in a bun, and she was still wearing her lavender waitress uniform.

Coach Bebop marched over to Mom and gruffly said, "Sorry ma'am, but this is a closed practice. We should be done shortly."

Coach Farmer jogged over and cried, "Bertha, where are your manners? Let Ms. O'Connell come onto the field. Her tax dollars are paying for your pension."

Coach Farmer turned to Mom and grinned. "Hey babe, to what do we owe the pleasure of this surprise visit?"

"Did Farmer just call your mom 'babe'?" Penelope asked.

"I didn't hear anything," I said nervously.

Mom held up her container. "I got off work a little early today, so I thought I'd drop off these cookies. I figured you guys would be hungry."

Coach grabbed the container. "You are the most thoughtful person I know. We would love to feast on your sugary delights. Wouldn't we, fellas?"

"Heck yeah!" hollered Heffer, thrusting his filthy hands into the container.

The Dunces started gorging on the cookies, too.

"Should we tell everyone your mom can't cook?" Abdul asked.

"Let them find out on their own," I replied with a devilish grin.

It only took a few seconds before people started gagging.

"These are nasty!" Rufus cried, wiping his mouth.

"I know, they're horrible!" Heffer hollered.

Mom lowered her head. "I'll be the first to admit I'm no Betty Crocker."

Coach Farmer's face turned fiery red. "Penny did a sweet thing making us cookies! I will not tolerate anyone disrespecting her culinary techniques!"

Coach Heffer and the Dunces shut up.

Farmer blew his whistle. "Gather around, everyone. I have an announcement."

The team surrounded Coach as he wiped his head with a handkerchief.

"Well gang, I have something I want to tell you. A few months ago I started seeing someone… Harold's mother, Penny."

All my teammates gasped. My friends turned to me with their mouths wide open. Jasper and Cletus stared at Shawn in horror.

I jumped up and said, "Haha, that's a good one, Coach. Now how about we head inside? I think the heat is messing with your brain."

Coach held out his hands. "Now now, Harold, I know you're probably just too modest to tell all your friends about how you're going to have an awesome new pappy."

"Do what?" Penelope hollered. All my teammates started whispering.

Shawn nervously said, "Okay Dad, enough goofing off. Let's go inside and---"

"Now son, there are no secrets amongst family, and I consider the entire William Henry Harrison Middle School faculty and student body to be my extended family. Last night I proposed to Penny O'Connell, and she said yes."

Everyone gasped again. My friends were stunned. Jasper had a disgusted look on his face. Shawn looked as sick as I felt.

In case anyone didn't believe Coach Farmer's shocking statement, Mom held up her tiny engagement ring.

"It's true," she gushed. "I'm about to have a new husband... and a new son."

Mom turned to Shawn and smiled. "Welcome to the family, Shawn."

A few guys chuckled. The rest of the team continued whispering. This was the biggest scandal in William Henry Harrison Middle School history. As soon as practice ended, everyone in town would know about it. A couple people had their phones out. Word was probably already being spread on Facebook and Twitter.

As if I wasn't embarrassed enough, Coach Farmer had to wrap his arms around Mom's waist and peck her on the lips.

Everyone shouted, "Ewww!" including Coach Bebop and Coach Heffer.

Coach Farmer turned to Coach Bebop. "I want you to be my best man, Bertha."

"You do realize I'm a woman, right?" Coach Bebop growled.

Coach Farmer scratched his head. "So women can't be best men?"

"What about me?" Coach Heffer asked.

"You can be one of Penny's bridesmaids," Coach Farmer replied.

"Wait, what?" Mom said.

Jasper leaned toward Shawn and said, "Why didn't you tell us about this?"

"I... I was embarrassed," Shawn stammered.

Jasper held up his hand and turned away. "I don't even want to hear it."

Shawn jumped up and started running off the field. Coach Farmer grabbed his jersey and yanked him back.

"Where you going, buddy? I didn't dismiss anyone yet."

"You embarrassed me in front of the entire team! I'm going to the car!"

Shawn tried to run again, but Coach Farmer held him in place.

"Sorry son, but you're not going home right away."

"What do you mean?" Shawn cried.

"Well, your soon-to-be mom and I thought you and Harold could have a study date this afternoon."

All my teammates burst out laughing.

"Aww, can we come to the study date, too, Fat-Man?" Ben cackled.

"Mom, what is Coach Farmer talking about?" I hollered.

Mom curled a few strands of hair around her finger, which she did whenever she was about to tell me something I wouldn't like. "Well Harold, as you know, you're not exactly the world's greatest student. And Shawn has a solid C-average."

Shawn and I hung our heads in shame as our teammates cackled.

"You see, son," Coach Farmer started to say, "Your mother and I just want..."

"I'm not your son!" I exploded.

Farmer's mouth dropped open in shock. All my teammates went, "Ohhhh...."

Mom glared at me. "Harold, go to the car! We'll talk about this later tonight."

"Shawn, go with Harold," Farmer ordered. "I'll pick you up later this evening, after your study date."

"Quit calling it that!" Shawn shouted.

Our teammates continued laughing as Shawn and I dashed to my mom's car. We left our dignity on the field.

Chapter Seven

Mom drove me, Shawn, and my friends home from practice. Normally that wouldn't be a big deal, because usually Granny picked us up in her minivan. But Mom drove a much smaller car. Since Shawn was Mom's 'soon-to-be-new-son', he got special treatment and was allowed to sit up front. The rest of us had to squeeze into the back. It was a very uncomfortable ride, especially because my friends kept cracking jokes about me and Shawn becoming brothers. I was thankful when Mom finally dropped them off. Soon it was just me, Mom, and Shawn.

Mom pulled into the driveway. Jon was chasing Anthony with the garden hose, spraying water everywhere.

Mom kicked open her door and shouted, "Knock it off! Get in the house!"

Jon threw down the hose and ran inside, giggling.

Anthony ran up to Mom in his underwear and hugged her legs.

"Hi Mommy!"

Mom smiled and picked him up.

"Hi baby." She wiped some caked mud off his cheeks. "Let's get you cleaned up, then yell at your grandmother for not watching you."

I grabbed the hose and turned it off before it carved a lake into our lawn. Shawn grinned for the first time all afternoon.

"The excitement never ends at the O'Connell household, huh?"

"Unfortunately not," I mumbled, tossing the leaky hose off to the side. "C'mon, let's go inside and get this over with."

Shawn and I walked into chaos. Granny and Great Granny were standing in the kitchen, bickering about something. I could barely hear them over all the noise, but it sounded like Granny got caught cheating while playing poker at the senior center again. Aunt Patty and Aunt Kathy were in the living room, sobbing uncontrollably over some Lifetime movie. Betty Beagle ran around in circles, barking so someone would give her a treat. Loud music blared from the basement, which meant Chucky was practicing with his grunge heavy metal band. And of course Jon and Anthony ran around the house in their underwear, screaming like maniacs.

"Sorry for all the craziness," I said. "I have to put up with this every day."

"Are you kidding me?" Shawn exclaimed. "This is amazing!"

"Wait, are you serious?" I sputtered.

"Yes," Shawn said. "I'd love to come home to a madhouse. My house is so quiet, sometimes I feel like I'm about to go insane."

"If we don't do something about our parents' wedding, then this *will* become your madhouse," I said gloomily.

"Uh, yeah, we can't let that happen," Shawn grumbled.

It may have been my imagination, but it almost seemed like Shawn was having second thoughts about our plan. "C'mon, let's go up to my room."

I led Shawn upstairs and down the cluttered hallway. Jon and Anthony had toys thrown all over the place. Skateboards, action figures, footballs, basketballs, you name it. It was a wonder my grannies hadn't fallen and broken a hip yet.

We finally reached my room, which was even messier than the hallway. I weaved through piles of dirty laundry and stacks of comic books, video game cartridges, and football cards. It looked like someone robbed Santa Claus and hid the loot in my room.

"Sorry for the mess," I said, clearing a spot off my bed.

"It's okay." Shawn pulled out my desk chair and plopped down.

We both sat there quietly for about a minute. For two guys who had exchanged countless insults over the years, we sure didn't have much to talk about.

Shawn picked up a comic. "Whoa, you like *Uncanny Mutant Commandos?*"

He grabbed another comic and exclaimed, "And *The Astonishing Chronicles of Tarantula-Boy?*"

"Yeah, those are my favorites," I replied.

"Mine too!" Shawn flipped through an issue of *Teenage Kung-Fu Cyborg Ferrets*. His grin grew wider.

"Dang, you have a lot. Some of these are classics."

Shawn held up an issue of *Tarantula-Boy*. "This is the first appearance of Rat-Dude." He then held up a copy of *Assassin Grandma*. "And this is when Assassin Grandma kills Dr. Platypus and hangs his charred corpse from the Statue of Liberty!"

I burst out laughing. "Yeah, those are some pretty awesome issues."

Shawn continued staring at my comics in wide-eyed wonder. "Some of these gotta be worth a ton of money. You should sell them. You'd make a killing!"

My face darkened. "My dad left me these comics. I'll never get rid of them. *Never.*"

Shawn looked up and frowned. "Oh. Sorry. I didn't mean anything by that."

I blinked away tears and shook my head. "Don't worry about it."

I wiped my eyes. The last thing I needed was to cry in front of my arch-nemesis.

"I miss my mom, too," Shawn said quietly. "She passed away when I was really young, but I remember a lot about her. She used to always hug and kiss me. I remember I used to hate that, but now... well, now I wish I could hug and kiss her. Just once."

I looked up at Shawn. A few tears ran down his cheeks.

I took a deep breath. "I know... it's hard. It's been hard on my whole family, especially my mom. Even though we have a houseful of people, I think she's still lonely. That's probably why she started seeing your dad."

Shawn looked up and met my gaze. I immediately felt bad for wanting to ruin Mom's engagement. Who was I to decide who she should and shouldn't see? But then I remembered how much I couldn't stand Coach Farmer, or Shawn. They were both so mean to me for so long. My tears instantly dried up and my face hardened.

"We should get started on our school work," I said coldly.

Shawn wiped his eyes. "Are you sure? Don't you want to play some video games first?"

"No, I think we should study and get this over with," I said bluntly, pulling my math book out of my bag.

"Oh. Okay." Shawn grabbed his book and knelt beside my bed.

We spent the next ten minutes trying to do our homework. Shawn really tried to help, but I just wasn't getting it. I might as well have been studying a foreign language.

"This is hopeless," I grumbled, closing my book. "I guess I'll just have to repeat the seventh grade for the rest of my life."

Shawn closed his book, too. "Let's take a break. We do have other things to do."

"Like what?"

"Like breaking up our parents' engagement. Do you have a laptop?"

"Yeah," I said, pulling my laptop out from under my bed. "It's an old one. It was my dad's, but my mom let me have it after... well, you know."

"It'll work." Shawn turned it on and pulled up a dating website I always saw commercials for late at night. He tapped away on my keyboard for a few seconds, then said, "There we go. I created two accounts, one for your mom and one for my dad."

"So are we going to upload pictures of our folks?" I asked.

Shawn chuckled. "Heck no. Our parents are old as dirt. No hot, young person will want to date them. I'll just use pics of attractive people I find on the internet. From what I've heard, everyone lies about what they look like on these things."

"I don't think this is going to work," I said gloomily.

"Relax, I'll handle everything," Shawn said. "I'll keep an eye on the profiles over the next few days and reply to everyone who responds. The richest, best-looking people will be the ones I choose. All you gotta do is convince your mom to ask my dad to take her to Uncle Bob's this Saturday. My dad will do whatever she asks."

"Uncle Bob's?" I said in disbelief. "Are you freaking kidding? We probably aren't allowed back in there after what happened with the pig."

"That was your granny's fault," Shawn pointed out. "He can't be mad at us."

"I guess you're right. It shouldn't be too hard to get my mom to want to go. She'll probably be thrilled that I want to be seen out in public with her."

"Great." Shawn clicked off the dating site and pulled up his Facebook account.

"What are you doing?" I asked.

"Helping you snag a date." Shawn scrolled through his friends list and clicked on April's profile. Her gorgeous face smiled at us from the computer screen.

My cheeks flushed. "How do you know I like... I mean, I don't like... I mean..."

Shawn smirked. "Don't embarrass yourself. I'd have to be an idiot not to realize you have the hots for April. I saw you hitting on her today during our softball game. By the way, your pickup lines need a lot of work."

I remembered Shawn staring at me when I bombed with April.

"Okay, so I like her. Is that a crime?"

"No, it means you have good taste. And I

want to help you."

My jaw dropped. "Why would you do that?"

Shawn shrugged. "I just hate seeing clueless guys embarrass themselves."

"I was stupid for talking to her anyway," I said, blushing. "A girl like that would never go for a slob like me."

"Sure she would. You just have to know what to say to her. You have to know what her interests are and act like *you're* interested. Didn't you ever look her up on Facebook to see what she liked?"

"I tried, but her personal info is blocked from public view. And I'm too chicken to send her a friend's request."

"Luckily for you, April is one of my Facebook friends. Here's all her private info."

That got me to shut up. I leaned over Shawn's shoulder and looked at her page.

"As you can see, her favorite women's soccer team is the Chicago Red Stars. She's also into the environment. So pretend you're a soccer-lover who likes to recycle."

"Gee, thanks," I said, patting Shawn on the back.

Shawn grinned. "See, I'm not as bad as people think."

"Maybe people wouldn't think that if you didn't have mean friends."

Shawn's smile faded away. "You mean the Dunces?"

"Duh. Why do you hang out with them? They can't be that fun to be around."

Shawn shrugged. "They used to be cool, but..."

Shawn trailed off. I just stared at him,

waiting for him to talk.

Shawn finally said, "It's hard to make new friends when you've been with the same pals since kindergarten. I've fought with so many people over the years..."

Shawn trailed off again. I knew exactly what he was getting at. He spent so many years treating people like scum that he was basically stuck with the Dunces. Now that Shawn was older, he probably realized just how awful he'd been over the years. But it was too late for him to fix his image. The damage was done.

Shawn twiddled his thumbs. "Look Harold, I..."

I never heard what he was about to say because Mom shouted up the stairs, "Dinner's ready! I made meatloaf!"

"Eat my mom's cooking at your own risk," I warned.

Shawn's smile returned. "If your family acts half as crazy as they did at Uncle Bob's, this is going to be a fun night.

With that, my 'once-mortal-enemy-but-now-sort-of-friend' and I made our way downstairs.

Chapter Eight

I thought dinner was pretty hectic, but Shawn seemed to enjoy himself. Coach Farmer stopped by, and Chucky's band mates Buster, Blade, and Diamond ate with us, so the table was packed.

I always liked when Chucky's friends joined us for dinner because they were just as cool as he was. All three of them had tons of body piercings and tattoos. Blade and Buster had cool mohawks. Diamond, the only girl in the band, had shaggy purple hair and an awesome fire-breathing dragon tattoo that ran all along her right arm. When they first started coming over for band practice, I think my family was scared of them. But now my mom and grannies treated them like they were their own kids.

Granny especially loved Diamond. She grabbed her arm and said, "I'm thinking about getting a dragon tattoo on my back. You should come with me to make sure it's done right."

"Sure thing, Granny," Diamond said with a grin.

Great Granny made the sign of the cross and whispered quotes from scripture.

As much as my family drove me crazy, the one thing I loved about them was how accepting they were. Anyone was allowed at our kitchen table, regardless of their age, race, orientation, or the number of tattoos they had.

For the first time since our parents announced their engagement, Shawn was relaxed and happy. He giggled the entire time. He especially cracked up when Betty jumped up on the table and scarfed down Great Granny's meatloaf. It was hilarious seeing Great Granny chase Betty all throughout the house.

Shawn also thought it was funny when Jon put his face in his potatoes, Chucky and his pals sang a couple verses from their school-inappropriate songs, Anthony threw food up at the ceiling fan (sending it flying everywhere), and my aunts bickered about the time Aunt Kathy cut off Aunt Patty's hair... when they were five. I personally would have rathered eaten upstairs in my room, but Shawn had a blast.

Shawn and Coach stayed until 10:00, which I found odd since it was a school night. I went to bed shortly afterwards, but I didn't fall asleep right away because I kept thinking about the wedding.

I was pretty tired when I went to school the next day. All the kids at the bus stop smirked when I walked over. It took me a few seconds to remember everyone knew about Coach Farmer proposing to Mom. A few guys cracked some jokes, but I ignored them. I was used to being picked on, so it didn't faze me.

Shawn, however, was *not* used to being harassed. I don't know what he expected, but I'm sure he never thought kids would laugh in his face. He had no more than walked over when Ben hollered, "Look everybody, Fat-man's new brother is here!"

Everyone laughed, including Shawn's pals. I expected my friends to make fun of Shawn, but I never thought *his* friends would.

I always thought Shawn was a tough guy, but he had never really been bullied before. At first he was shocked by all the jokes and insults. That gave way to humiliation. Soon he was on the verge of tears.

I couldn't take it anymore. I hated it when I got picked on. I couldn't stand back and not say anything. That would make me a hypocrite.

"Knock it off, guys. He's had enough."

Everyone looked at me funny. One of Shawn's pals finally said, "Did you hear that? The biggest nerd in school is sticking up for Shawn."

"That means Shawn is a bigger nerd than Harold," another guy cackled.

Shawn's friends snickered and walked away. I instantly felt bad. By sticking up for Shawn, I accidentally made things worse.

Without looking up, Shawn mumbled, "Thanks Harold." He then walked over to a tree and leaned against it. Shawn was usually surrounded by tons of people. Seeing him alone was a weird sight.

Ben slapped me on the back. "What's wrong with you, Fat-man? After everything Shawn's said to us over the years, we're finally getting some payback."

"Yeah," Blake said. "He was about to cry. Why'd you make us stop?"

"Two wrongs don't make a right," I said, borrowing one of my mom's favorite sayings. She said it every time I hit Jon after he made me mad.

My friends shook their heads and walked away.

Ms. Spear pulled up to the bus stop a few seconds later. "Hurry up, hoodlums!" she shrieked. "I'm missing my morning talk shows!"

We all scurried onto the bus. I sat with Jon and my friends up front. I turned around and watched Shawn make his way to the back. Kids taunted him along the way. But that was nothing compared to what happened when he reached the backseat. His friends actually refused to let him sit down.

"C'mon guys, I always sit here," Shawn said. "Let me squeeze in."

One of Shawn's pals said, "Why don't you go sit with your new geeky brother?"

The rest of Shawn's pals snickered. Shawn looked directly at me and frowned. I felt bad, but my friends would go crazy if I let him sit with us.

The bus jerked forward, causing Shawn to stumble. His pals laughed even harder.

Ms. Spear muttered, "What the...." and slammed on the brakes. This made Shawn fall flat on his butt.

"Sit down, hoodlum!" Mrs. Spear screamed. "I can't drive if you're standing!"

Shawn jumped up and said, "But..."

"SIT DOWN!"

Shawn gulped and plopped down next to a couple members of the chess club. Ironically, they called *him* a nerd. The world had gone topsy-turvy.

Things didn't get much better for Shawn once we got to school. He continued to get picked on during Ms. Hornswaggle's class. He was obviously not used to kids making fun of him because he looked frazzled. I shook my head in silent pity. His skin wasn't thick enough for him to be taunted mercilessly. He wouldn't last a week if it continued.

The rest of the class filed in and plopped down at their desks. I anxiously waited for April to come in. English was the only class besides gym that I shared with her. I hoped she didn't remember how stupid I acted the day before.

April finally skipped into the room humming a Dustin Bopper song. I was too disgusted to be excited. I seriously hated Dustin Bopper. He was this puny little 15-year old pop singer with 'perfect, wind-swept hair' and the 'voice of an angel'. (Those aren't my words, by the way. I'm quoting *Tigerbeat*. Like most guys, I couldn't stand the dude.)

Ever since Dustin Bopper became a pop sensation, girls have expected the rest of us dudes to copy his dweeby haircut. A few guys did just to make their girlfriends happy. I, however, had too much self-respect to do that. Although… if that was the only thing preventing April from going out with me, I *might* consider it. But other than that, I had too much self-respect.

Even more disturbing than April humming Dustin Bopper, however, was the fact that she was carrying a copy of *Blood-Red Sunrise*. *Blood-Red Sunrise* was a horribly written series of paranormal teen novels about vampires, zombies, and werewolves. They weren't cool vampires and zombies, either, but a bunch of wusses who all fell in love with this whiny, helpless girl named Selma. I read the first page of the first book two years ago to see why girls loved it so much. I seriously about vomited halfway through the first paragraph. I had too much self-respect to read another single page of *Blood-Red Sunrise*, or to watch a second of one of the movies. Although… if me pretending to like *Blood-Red Sunrise* would get April to like me, I would seriously consider it. But other than that, I had too much self-respect.

When I turned around, I was surprised to see Penelope glaring at me. She quickly turned away when I saw her. Something weird was going on with that girl.

The bell finally rang. Seconds later, Ms. Hornswaggle wobbled in with Ms. Meow Meow. Everyone stopped talking so we didn't upset Hornswaggle's demon kitty.

While Ms. Hornswaggle scribbled our lesson plan up on the chalkboard, I gazed out the window and struggled to stay awake. I was just about to doze off when I heard the familiar sound of a spitball splattering against human flesh. I yelped and jumped out of my seat. Everyone turned around and stared at me.

Ms. Hornswaggle peered at me over the top of her bifocals. "Do you have something you wish to contribute to our literary conversation, Mr. O'Connell?"

"No thanks." I touched my cheek and was shocked to find it perfectly dry. That's when I noticed Shawn looking frantically around the room. He must have been the target.

I spent the rest of the class keeping an eye out for spit-ballers. Several guys took aim at the back of Shawn's head, and the most shocking part was that they were all his buddies. Poor Shawn got blasted with over a dozen spitballs within a matter of minutes. Part of me was glad I wasn't the target, but the other part, the *good* part, felt bad.

Shawn eventually got a detention for yelping too much. My classmates and I were stunned. Shawn never got a detention. *Never.* Shawn tried to explain to Ms. Hornswaggle that people were hitting him with spitballs, but she didn't believe him. She claimed popular kids like him never got picked on.

When Shawn got splattered with yet another spitball, I knew I'd had enough. I couldn't leave a fellow dweeb to fend for himself, even if he used to be my most bitter arch-nemesis. I whipped out a straw, loaded it with a spitball, and let it fly. One of the guys tormenting Shawn jumped out of his seat and yelped.

That was the good news. The bad news was, Ms. Meow Meow had seen the entire thing. She ran up to me and hissed.

Ms. Hornswaggle crossed her jiggly arms. "Are you the one who's been shooting spitballs, Mr. O'Connell?"

"No," I said, dropping my straw under my desk. Stupid Ms. Meow Meow picked it up with her mouth and ran over to Ms. Hornswaggle.

Ms. Hornswaggle grabbed the straw and twirled it around in her hand.

"Are you calling my kitty a liar?" she snarled.

"Yes!" I exclaimed. "Your cat has mental issues. And so do you."

I immediately threw my hands over my mouth. I was always blurting out things that I shouldn't. I got it from my granny.

The entire class burst out laughing as Ms. Hornswaggle's face turned scarlet. She whipped out a pink piece of paper and bellowed, "DETENTION!"

I groaned and banged my head against my desk.

Chapter Nine

Usually lunch was my favorite part of the day. But this was a rare occasion when I did not enjoy it. There were two reasons. One, we had vegetable potpie. That was even worse than vegetable lasagna. And two, my friends kept harassing me about my mom's engagement to Coach Farmer.

"Seriously dude, you can't let your mom go through with this," Penelope said with a mouthful of potpie. (I let her have mine.) "Your home life will be ruined if Shawn and his dad live with you."

"It can't be worse than it already is," Abdul chuckled. "What with his wacky grannies, aunts, and 12-year old uncle, it's a wonder he hasn't already lost his marbles."

"At least my family doesn't make me pray all day when I'm home," I snapped.

Abdul got red in the face. I immediately felt bad. "Sorry Abdul," I grumbled. "You know I like your parents. I'm just really stressed out about the wedding."

"Don't worry, Fat-Man," Ben said, patting me on the back. "Things will work out. But I do have one question. When Coach becomes your new daddy, will your name change to Harold Farmer?"

I felt the color drain from my face.

"Oh no, I didn't even think about that," I gasped.

My friends cackled like hyenas on a sugar-high.

While my pals made fun of my new last name, I glanced around the lunch room. Coach Farmer was up front yelling at some kids for throwing garbage at his head. I looked in the back and saw April chatting with her soccer pals. My stomach twisted into a knot as I thought about my plans to ask April out. The more I thought about it, the more nervous I got. So I stopped thinking.

That's when I noticed Shawn walking out of the lunch line. I watched as Shawn uneasily made his way over to the Dunces' table. Jasper, Rufus, and Cletus were smacking each other and laughing obnoxiously. That was about as civilized as they acted out in public. They became quiet when Shawn appeared.

"Er, hey guys," Shawn said awkwardly.

The Dunces and their pals stared at Shawn like he was wearing a giant diaper.

Shawn started to sit down, but stopped when he realized there was no room.

"C'mon Rufus, you goofball, scoot over," Shawn said.

"Duh, okay." Rufus started to move, but Jasper shoved him back.

Jasper looked down and played with his food. "Sorry Shawn, there's no room."

"There's plenty of room," Shawn said, his forehead glistening with sweat. "We always sit together. Scoot over."

"Maybe we don't want you sitting with us no more," Jasper said.

"W… why?" Shawn stuttered. It was painful to watch, it really was.

Jasper sighed and finally looked up. "Do we really have to point it out to you?"

Jasper pointed at me. I gulped and turned away.

"That's why," I heard Jasper say. "Why don't you go sit with your geeky new brother?"

Jasper's entire table erupted in laughter. I was no longer looking in their direction, so I just assumed Shawn went to a different table on the far side of the room. I was therefore shocked when he popped up in front of me, right behind Penelope.

"Hey guys," Shawn said uneasily.

My friends stopped talking and looked up in astonishment. Food fell out of Blake's gaping mouth.

Penelope jumped up and pounded her fist into her palm. "What do you want, Farmer? If you came over her to cause trouble, I'll..."

Shawn said, "No, you got it all wrong. I wanted to sit with you guys."

Penelope was never caught speechless, but Shawn's shocking statement did the impossible. She looked over at me and cocked an eyebrow.

Not knowing what else to say, I replied, "Sure, we have plenty of room."

"Do what?" my friends exploded simultaneously.

"Are you freaking kidding me?" Penelope cried. "Shawn's been treating us like dirt since kindergarten, and now all of a sudden you expect us to like him?"

"Uh...," I started to say.

"You actually think we're gonna sit with Farmer, Fat-Man?" Ben hollered. "You're even dumber than you look."

"Er..."

"My parents are always telling me how I should forgive my enemies, but even I can't forgive

Shawn for years of nastiness," Abdul said.

"Well…"

"Are you going to eat your chocolate cake?" Blake asked loudly.

Everyone stared at Blake. His hearing aid was obviously malfunctioning again.

Shawn continued standing behind Penelope, silently fuming as he was bombarded with insults. He really must not have had anywhere else to go.

"We are not sitting with Shawn," Penelope growled, drawing a line in the sand. "It's either us, your best pals… or him, your worst enemy."

Penelope pointed at Shawn. Shawn responded by sticking out his tongue.

I obviously liked my friends 100-times more than Shawn, but I hated when people tried to boss me around. So I stubbornly said, "Fine, go sit somewhere else."

Penelope gasped. I had clearly taken her by surprise.

Ben shook his head. "Not cool, Fat-Man. Not cool."

Ben, Abdul, and Penelope grabbed their trays and walked away. Blake looked around and asked, "Where's everyone going?"

Penelope grabbed Blake by his shirt and dragged him to an empty table.

Shawn sat down where Penelope had been sitting and stared at his food.

"Thanks," he mumbled. "Sorry I made your friends leave."

"Don't worry, they'll get over it by tomorrow," I said. "We fight from time to time, but never for more than a day or two."

Shawn took a sip of milk and said, "Yeah, that's how my friends are sometimes. They're giving me a hard time about the wedding, but we'll be back to normal by tomorrow." He took another sip and murmured, "Or maybe the day after tomorrow."

I doubted that. I didn't want to be the one to burst Shawn's bubble, but his days of hanging with the Dunces were over. He'd have to find that out on his own, though.

"So anyway, we already got some hits on that dating site," Shawn said.

I spun around and grinned. "Really?"

"Yep. Apparently there are a lot of sad, lonely people out there. We got 20 messages. 18 were for your mom and two were for my dad. I guess there are more men looking for women than the other way around."

I shrugged. "Makes sense I guess."

Shawn laid a bunch of photos on the table. "I printed up some of the profiles so you can see what we're dealing with. I've gotta warn you, it isn't pretty."

I cracked up when I saw some of the people who e-mailed my mom. Most of the guys were super-old (like over 40) and super fat. One guy had a mullet, another guy had a horrible comb-over, and another dude only had three teeth. Mom was pretty desperate, but not *that* desperate.

Even worse than the guys' appearances, though, was the fact that most of them were on disability, or worked part-time at Waffle House. Not that there's anything wrong with working at Waffle House; that's my dream job! And my grannies got social security, so I didn't care about that, either. But the whole point of using a dating site was so I could find my mom someone who was younger, hotter, and richer than Coach Farmer. As much as it pained me to admit it, Farmer blew most of the dating site dudes out of the water... except for one.

"Oh, he looks promising," I said, picking up the photo of a 24-year old blond-haired, pre-med surfer dude.

"That's Chad Michaels." Shawn grabbed all the other photos and shuffled them.

I put the photo down on the table. "Now wait a minute, why would someone like Chad Michaels want to date my mom? She's a lot older than he is."

"She's not old, she's only 22."

"Yeah right. Add about 10 years and you're almost there."

"That's not what her profile says." Shawn handed me Mom's profile, except the woman in the photo wasn't Mom. It was some young, gorgeous girl with long, black hair. Mom's bio claimed she was a lingerie model and an aspiring actress.

I groaned. "That's an image I'll never get out of my head."

"If you think that's weird, you should get a load of my dad." Shawn passed me another profile. It was Shawn's dad, except the guy in the picture looked nothing like him. The new and improved Coach Farmer looked like a bodybuilder with muscles popping out all over the place. His bio was even more ridiculous. It said Coach was a former Mr. Universe contestant, a scientist who used to work at the CERN particle accelerator in Switzerland, and a current college professor who taught courses on quantum mechanics. I had no idea what CERN was, and I definitely knew nothing about quantum mechanics. I was pretty sure Coach Farmer didn't, either.

I burst out laughing so hard, people at nearby tables looked over at us (including my friends and the Dunces).

"You two having fun on your lunch date?" Jasper cackled.

Shawn lowered his head and got all quiet.

"Ignore them," I mumbled. "I do all the time."

Shawn blinked his moist eyes until they dried up. Speaking much quieter than he did before, he said, "So as you can see, I pretended my dad likes to work out. The weird thing is, the girls who e-mailed him were more interested in him being a scientist."

"That is weird. So are the girls who e-mailed your dad young and hot?"

Shawn made a face. "No. They're both super old and neither have a good job."

"Rats," I grumbled.

"Don't panic yet," Shawn said. "We still have a couple days until the weekend. And remember, it just takes one to stop a wedding. As long as Chad woos your mom, we're good. I'll send him a message later saying your mom wants to meet him Saturday night. You just work on getting your mom to take us to Uncle Bob's."

"I'll ask her tonight," I said.

I took a deep breath and exhaled. I was just beginning to feel cautiously optimistic about our crazy plan.

That's when a sweaty, meaty hand clamped down on my shoulder. I spun around, expecting to find a Dunce towering over me. Instead I found Coach Farmer.

"Now isn't this just precious," Coach Farmer bellowed. I nervously glanced around.

Everyone within hearing range stared at us.

Shawn chuckled nervously. "Dad, don't embarrass us."

Coach Farmer blew raspberries. "Don't worry, son. You know I'm a cool, hip dad. I won't do anything to embarrass you guys. I'm just glad my two little men are finally acting like loving brothers. Your mother will be so proud when I tell her."

Shawn groaned and buried his head in his arms as people around us laughed.

"You and my mom aren't even married yet," I said through gritted teeth. "So you need to quit acting like my mom is Shawn's mom. She's not."

Coach Farmer cackled and slapped me on the back so hard that I nearly fell face-first into my applesauce. "I see what's going on here. You don't wanna share your momma. Don't worry, son, there's plenty of her to go around. And I don't care if we aren't married yet, I still want you to call me your pappy."

"Dad!" Shawn wailed.

Thankfully Coach Farmer had the attention of a beagle puppy in a flower-filled meadow. A kid threw a paper airplane and he ran after it.

"That was extremely painful," I muttered.

"Now you see what I always have to put up with," Shawn grumbled. "And remember, at home it's just me and him. I get the full brunt of his craziness."

"You have my sympathy," I said.

I had hoped things would calm down for a bit, but that turned out to be a pipe dream. Coach had no more than walked away when a carton of milk exploded against the back of my head, drenching me from head to toe. Some of the milk splattered on Shawn.

I spun around and glared at the Dunces, who were cackling like crazy. I was about to return fire, but Shawn grasped my wrist and said, "Allow me."

Shawn stood up, grabbed his milk, and chucked it at Jasper. The carton seemed to fly through the air in slow motion. A stream of milk shot out of the carton as it whizzed toward its target, making it look like the fiery white tail of a blazing comet.

Jasper had just turned around from hi-fiving Cletus when the carton smashed against his face. Milk splattered everywhere, getting Jasper even more soaked than I was.

Jasper wiped his eyes and glared at me. Then he looked behind me and gasped. Shawn was still standing tall, smiling triumphantly.

"You'll pay for that, Farmer," Jasper snarled. "Sic em, Rufus."

Rufus scratched his bald head. "Duh, okay."

Rufus grabbed his slice of cherry pie and hurled it at Shawn's head. Unfortunately for Rufus, Coach Farmer had just walked back over and stopped directly in his line of fire. The slice of pie splattered all over Coach's face. Shawn and I covered our mouths to dampen our squeals of laughter.

Coach wiped his eyes. "What in tarnation is the matter with you Dunces?"

"I'm sorry, Coach!" Rufus cried. "I wasn't tryin' ta hit you, I was-mmm!"

Jasper threw his hand over Rufus' mouth. "What my goofy cousin is trying to say, Coach, is that he was trying to give his pie to your son, but he tripped. The pie flew out of his hand and accidentally hit you."

Coach Farmer tapped his foot. He obviously didn't believe Jasper's lame story.

He certainly didn't believe it after Rufus blubbered, "But Jasper, I didn't trip."

"Meet me in my office, Rufus!" Farmer snapped.

Rufus dashed out of the cafeteria, bawling like a baby.

Coach turned to me and said, "Holy mackerel! What happened to you, son?"

With all the craziness, I nearly forgot I'd been drenched with milk. I grinned at the sight of Jasper mouthing, *"Don't even think about it."*

That made me want to do it even more. "Coach, Jasper was trying to hit Shawn with a milk carton, but I jumped in the way to save him."

Coach's eyes welled up with tears. With a trembling bottom lip, he said, "You risked your life for my son. I'll never be able to repay you."

I rubbed the back of my head and said, "I don't think Shawn was ever in any danger, unless he's lactose-intolerant."

Coach ignored me and pointed a quivering finger at Jasper.

"Why did you try to take out my boy?"

"I didn't, Coach!" Jasper stammered. "I was trying to hit Harold!"

Coach scoffed. "So it's not enough for you to go after my biological son, you also gotta go after my new stepson? Why don't you and Cletus join Rufus in my office?

Cletus burst into tears like his goofy brother. Jasper rolled his eyes and led his hysterical cousin to Coach's office.

Coach Farmer eventually ran after another paper airplane.

Shawn leaned toward me and said, "You know the Dunces aren't going to take this lying down. They're going to get back at you somehow, someway."

"I could say the same to you," I replied.

"W... what do you mean?" Shawn stammered.

I sighed and said, "The Dunces already hate me. But you were their best friend."

"What do you mean 'were'?" Shawn asked. The guy was in total denial.

"Shawn, after today you're no longer part of the Dunce's clique. In their eyes you betrayed them by sitting with me, sticking up for me, and getting them in trouble. From now on I'll probably be more of a friend than they will, and I can't stand you."

That, of course, was not entirely true. I was actually beginning to warm up to my arch-nemesis. But I couldn't let him know that. The entire reason we were trying to ruin our parents' wedding was because we *didn't* like each other. Admitting I kind of liked Shawn now would just complicate things. I still didn't want Coach Farmer walking around my house in an open bathrobe. It was bad enough my granny did that.

"You don't know what you're talking about," Shawn grumbled, picking at his potpie. He didn't sound like he believed his own words. And even if he did, he would soon see how wrong he was. You don't turn on your friends without there being fall-out.

Chapter Ten

The locker room was surprisingly peaceful. The Dunces were nowhere to be seen, so my friends and I were able to change without fear of being smacked with a wet towel. I could tell Shawn was happy when he walked in and saw his old pals M.I.A. Even though he didn't admit it, I knew my warning about the Dunces had startled him.

After we changed, we all went up to the gym and plopped down on our assigned spots on the floor. When April walked by, I took a deep breath and exhaled. She smelled like strawberries and lavender soup. Almost all girls smelled fruity and soapy. It was us guys who smelled like sweat socks and moldy cheese. I knew that from all the times I hung out with Blake and Abdul on hot, sticky, summer afternoons.

I smiled and waved at April, hoping to thaw the ice. She responded with an eye-roll and a flip of her long, red hair. Not only did I fail to thaw the ice, but now it had turned into an iceberg big enough to sink ten Titanics.

Coach Bebop and Coach Heffer barged out of their offices a few minutes later. Coach Heffer had a hard-hat on, I guess in case he got hit with a softball again.

Coach Bebop blew her whistle. "Alright gang, get off your booties and do some stretches. We're playing softball again."

Halfway through our stretches, Coach

Farmer burst through the gym doors with the Dunces. Coach Heffer hurried over.

"I was wondering where you Dunces were," Heffer said breathlessly. "I was worried sick."

"I had to give them a talking-to, Mark," Coach Farmer explained. "They tried to start a food fight with my son."

Coach Heffer gasped. "I expected more out of you Dunces. Wasting food like that when there are starving kids in Africa and famished gym teachers in America."

Coach Heffer patted his morbidly obese belly. I think he passed some gas because the stench of rotten eggs entered my nostrils.

Coach Farmer wagged his finger in Jasper's face. "I expect you and your cousins to be on your best behavior. Don't make me come back down here."

Coach Farmer waved at me and Shawn, then stormed out of the gym.

Coach Bebop blew her whistle and made us run outside into the horrible sunshine.

"My eyes!" Blake screamed, covering his glasses.

Coach Bebop blew her whistle in Blake's hearing aid. "Quit whining and move!"

We all jogged over to the softball field. Just like the day before, Shawn's team had all the star players, minus Penelope, while we had all the untalented, uncoordinated kids, plus Penelope.

"Play ball!" Coach Bebop screamed.

Penelope wound up her arm and hurled a fast-ball at Cletus' head. Cletus yelped and dropped to the ground.

"Strike one!" Coach Bebop shrieked gleefully.

Cletus scrambled to his feet. "Penelope just tried to kill me!"

"Quit being a baby," snapped Coach Bebop.

Penelope zipped the ball over home-plate a second time. Cletus swung a split-second later and spun around in a complete circle before falling flat on his butt. A cloud of dust shot into the air.

"Strike two!" Coach Bebop cackled.

Cletus pushed himself up with his bat and trembled in fear as Penelope wound up her arm a third time. When she finally threw it, Cletus screamed and dropped to the ground.

"Next!" Coach Bebop hollered.

April grabbed Cletus' bat and bent over home plate. The butterflies in my stomach started crashing into each other. Sweat poured from my armpits and I struggled not to vomit. The power girls had over boys was astonishing.

My mind raced as April waited for Penelope to make her first pitch. This was my one shot. If I didn't talk to April today, I probably never would. I'd forget all the cool stuff Shawn told me to say, and I'd continue to get more nervous. I just hoped April didn't hit the ball so far that she made it to third base. I couldn't very well have a romantic conversation with her on the other side of the baseball diamond.

Penelope wound up her arm and hurled the softball faster than I'd ever seen. Somehow April managed to hit it. Like last time, the ball flew toward second base. And like last time, I dropped to the ground and covered my head. Out of the corner of my eyes, I saw Coach Heffer get clonked on the head. He collapsed to the ground in a motionless heap. His hard-hat rolled next to me.

I groggily stood up. April raced toward me.

"Harold you bonehead, get the ball!" Penelope screamed.

I snatched the ball off the ground and ran toward second base just as April slid across. A cloud of dust shot into the air, making me cough.

April got up and wiped dirt off her shorts.

"Sorry," she mumbled.

I giggled and said, "Don't worry about it, you're an amazing ball player."

April looked up and smirked. "Didn't we have a similar conversation yesterday?"

I rubbed the back of my head and muttered, "Yeah, we did."

Penelope hollered, "Throw me the freaking ball, Harold!"

I twirled around and tossed the ball to Penelope. I then turned back to April and said, "Sooo... how are you?"

April rolled her eyes. "Buzz off, Harold. We're in the middle of a game."

I bit my trembling bottom lip. My last, best chance to win over the love of my life was quickly slipping away. I had to do something, and fast.

Throwing caution to the wind, I blurted out, "I wish people would stop chopping down the rainforests."

April looked at me suspiciously. "What did you say?"

"I was just saying I wish people would stop destroying the rainforests. It's bad. I think."

I had no idea what I was talking about. I really should have done some research about the rainforests so I didn't sound like an idiot.

I figured April would tell me to buzz off again. So I was surprised when she said, "Harold, I had no idea you cared about the environment.

That's my passion!"

"Really?" I said, pretending to be shocked. "I had no idea. That's my biggest passion, too. People should take better care of the planet. After all, we only have one."

April's grin became a full-fledged smile. "That's so weird. I have the exact same quote on my Facebook page."

"That is weird. It's almost like I stalked you online for hours on end, learning everything I could just to impress you."

April frowned. "Wait, what?"

"I mean, how about them Chicago Red Stars? That's my favorite soccer team."

April's smile returned. "Get out, mine too!"

We continued chatting for a minute or so while Penelope struck out Jasper. April rambled on about a bunch of soccer players I never heard of, then she talked about some endangered wildlife I didn't even knew existed. I just did what I always did whenever a hot girl talked to me; I smiled and nodded. So she thought I was smart, I occasionally said, *"Oh, I agree,"* and, *"Exactly, I couldn't have said it better myself!"*

April and I must have been louder than I thought because Penelope eventually spun around and hollered, "Be quiet, I can't concentrate!"

"Er, sorry," I said.

Penelope growled and went back to hurling balls at Shawn.

"I seriously don't know what's gotten into her lately," I grumbled to April.

"Ain't it obvious?" Coach Heffer said, wobbling over. He finally got up after getting whacked upside the back of the head.

"What you talkin' about, Heffer?" I asked.

"Dang boy, you must be s…s…stupid not to see Penelope has a crush on you. She's jealous of all the attention you're giving April."

April blushed.

"You're crazy, Coach," I said. "Penelope doesn't like me."

"Yeah she does," Heffer hollered for the entire world to hear. "She likes you a lot."

"I do not," Penelope hollered back. She twirled around and chucked the ball at us. April and I fell to the ground. Coach Heffer was too slow. He got thwacked upside the back of the head again, this time without his hard-hat. He collapsed to the ground.

Coach Bebop blew her whistle. "Penelope, home plate is over here! Concentrate!"

"Sorry Coach," Penelope grumbled.

April was still on the ground, so I helped her up.

"You like soccer, you care about the environment, and you're a gentleman," April said, beaming. "You're a man after my own heart."

I giggled again. "Aw shucks."

Penelope growled and chucked another ball at Shawn's head.

Coach Bebop clapped. "Good job, Penelope. You pitch like that this spring and we'll win the softball league championship for sure. Alright gang, let's change her up."

I groaned as everyone switched places on the field. My time to woo April had come to a close. I wanted to ask April if she wanted to hang out sometime, but my words got stuck in my throat.

"Well Harold, it was nice talking to you," April said.

I cleared my throat and hoarsely replied,

"Yeah, same here."

We were both quiet for a few seconds. April opened her mouth to say something, but then her friend Phoebe dashed over and said, "Catch, April."

Phoebe tossed April a glove. She then started chatting with her about something that happened at their soccer game the other day. It may have been my imagination, but it almost seemed like April was peeved that Phoebe interrupted us.

Blake said, "C'mon Harold, Bebop's gonna yell at us if we don't hurry."

I sighed and followed Blake over to the bench. Like yesterday our team got destroyed. And it was hot, so I sweated up a storm. I was super excited when Coach Bebop blew her whistle and ordered us to go inside.

We all filed past Coach Heffer, who was still sprawled out on the ground. I think I heard him mumble, "I've fallen and I can't get up," but I didn't stop to make sure. Coach Bebop kicked him to make sure he was still alive and walked away.

I knew Penelope was still mad because she didn't come over to talk to me. Ben, Abdul, and Blake did, though.

"What did you and April talk about, Fat-Man?" Ben asked excitedly.

Abdul rubbed his hands together. "Yeah, don't leave out any juicy details."

"My belly button smells like cheese," Blake said.

We all ignored our deaf friend.

I zipped my lips and threw away the key. "A gentleman never kisses and tells."

"Whatever, Fat-Man," Ben said. "You've never kissed a girl in your life."

"And your mom and grannies don't count,"

Abdul giggled.

"I wonder what cat food tastes like," Blake said loudly.

Ben, Abdul, and I gave Blake funny looks and walked away. I was in the middle of telling my disbelieving friends that I had, in fact, kissed several girls (even though I hadn't) when April hurried up to me and said, "Hi."

My jaw dropped. Ben and Abdul stared at April like she was a goddess.

April glanced at Ben and Abdul. "Are your friends okay? They're kind of freaking me out."

Ben grinned. "Hello gorgeous."

"You're awfully perty," Abdul gushed.

I shoved my friends away and told them I'd catch up with them later. I then turned back to April and did my best to sound cool.

"S'up?"

April fidgeted with her fingers, something I'd never seen her do before. Several of her friends stood off to the side, watching. Most of them looked disgusted.

Still fidgeting, April said, "I was, uh, wondering... well you see, I have these two tickets to see Dustin Bopper next Tuesday, and I..."

I instinctively stuck out my tongue. "Yuck."

April cocked an eyebrow. "You don't like Dustin Bopper?"

I couldn't help myself. "Heck no!" I hollered. "He sucks!"

April's face turned bright red. "Excuse me? He is incredibly talented. And he's so hot. How could you not like him?"

April put up her hand. "You know what? Forget it. I was going to ask you to take me to the concert."

My heart jumped into my throat. "Wait, what?"

April didn't hear me, she was still going off on a tirade. "My boyfriend was going to go with me, but we broke up last week. I was hoping you would go with me, but if you're going to start bad-mouthing Dustin then…"

"I'd love to go," I blurted out.

April stopped rambling. "Really?"

"Sure! I love Dustin Bopper! I, uh, thought you were talking about someone else."

April calmed down. "Oh, okay. Well, come pick me up at my house next Tuesday around seven."

"Sure. It's a date!"

April grinned. "Yeah, I guess it is."

April ran over to her friends. I overheard Phoebe tell April she couldn't believe she asked me out, that I was fat and gross. April didn't seem to care, though. She was still hopping up and down in excitement.

I glanced around and was surprised to see a bunch of people had stopped to watch me during my finest hour. Ben, Abdul, and some of the other guys rushed over to give me props. Shawn flashed me a thumbs-up. Even the Dunces seemed impressed. Penelope, though, was nowhere to be seen. I started to think maybe Coach Heffer was right about her liking me. I wasn't sure how I felt about that.

I did, however, know how I felt about April. By snagging a date with the hottest girl in school, my life was about to change dramatically… for the better.

At least, that's what I hoped!

Chapter Eleven

Coach Farmer really thought we stood a decent chance of beating Hoover Middle School Friday afternoon, as did the rest of the team. So everyone was understandably heartbroken when we lost 42-0. Coach locked himself in his office so he could cry. The rest of us just went home.

When I woke up the next morning and went downstairs for breakfast, Mom said, "There's my future NFL star."

I rolled my eyes. "First of all, Mom, we lost 42-0. Secondly, I sat on the bench the entire time!"

"Oh, I'm sure Michael Jordan sat on the bench from time to time," Mom said, wiping down the stove.

"Michael Jordan played basketball," I pointed out.

Mom ignored me. "I'm excited about our little double date later."

Granny spit out her coffee. "Double date? Does that mean Shawn is Harold's date?"

Granny kept on laughing while I rolled my eyes again and made a bowl of cereal. After that I did my Saturday morning chores and played video games until it was time to go to Uncle Bob's. I threw on jeans and a flannel shirt, but Mom went all out. She did her hair, put on perfume and makeup, and wore a blue dress. She was taking the whole dinner thing super serious. That was a good thing, though. Mom needed to put on as much mascara as possible if she was going to woo Chad Michaels.

Just before Mom and I were about to head out, the aunts came over to babysit Jon and Anthony. No one else was home. Chucky was out with his friends, and my grannies went to the senior center for their weekly chicken dinner bingo night.

Mom and I met Shawn and Coach Farmer in Uncle Bob's parking lot. While Mom looked like she was going to a ball, Coach Farmer looked like he belonged in the mosh pit of a rock concert. He had on a baseball cap, jean shorts, sandals, and a professional wrestling t-shirt.

"You look... nice," Mom said uneasily.

"My mom's being nice," I said to Shawn. "Your dad looks ridiculous."

"Hey, you're lucky I convinced him to wear a shirt," Shawn said.

"Whatever," I mumbled. "Let's get this over with."

Shawn and I followed our parents into the restaurant. It looked pretty crowded, but luckily there wasn't a line. The usher glanced at us and gasped.

"I think she remembers us from the other night," I whispered.

The usher whipped out a walkie-talkie. "Uncle Bob, we have a code red. I repeat, this is a code red."

"Oh dear, that doesn't sound good," Mom murmured.

Uncle Bob waddled over a few seconds later. He was still wearing his trademark overalls. Oinky scurried over with him and squealed when he saw us.

Uncle Bob's face turned fiery red. "You all

have a lot of nerve coming in here after the chaos you caused earlier this week."

"But that wasn't us, that was my 5-year old son and senile 62-year old mother," Mom pointed out. "Please let us eat here, we really enjoy the food."

"Especially the pork ribs," Coach said, licking his lips.

Oinky squealed at the mention of pork ribs. For all we knew, Coach could've eaten poor Oinky's brother the other night.

Uncle Bob's face softened. "I guess you're right. You weren't the ones who yanked tablecloths off my tables and caused little Oinky to have a nervous breakdown. And anyone who enjoys my ribs is okay in my book. I guess I don't see the harm in---"

The front door suddenly flew open and a familiar voice hollered, "There's a bunch of cranky, hungry grannies coming through! Everyone get out of the way if you know what's good for ya!"

I watched in horror as Granny, Great Granny, and over 30 of their blue-haired granny friends wobbled into the restaurant. Oinky left a present on the floor.

"Mother, what are you doing here?" Mom asked, not sounding too happy.

"We just got done with bingo, so me and the girls decided to get a bite to eat."

"Didn't you guys eat chicken?" I asked.

"What, we're not allowed to eat more than once?" Granny snapped. She pushed me out of the way and waddled up to the usher. "We need a table for 30, please."

Granny looked down at Oinky and smiled. "Hello Piggy. Remember me?"

Oinky squealed and ran over to Uncle Bob. Uncle Bob picked him up and caressed his head.

"No, absolutely not. I refuse to serve you and your raucous friends."

Great Granny waved her fist in the air. "How dare you refuse to seat us, whippersnapper!"

Granny said, "Let me handle this, Mother. Dr. Vangingle told you to watch your blood pressure."

She turned back to Uncle Bob. "You better serve us, buster. If you don't, we'll go to the media about age discrimination."

Uncle Bob's jaw dropped. "Wait, what?"

"You heard me. I'll call up Channel 5 News. I have them on speed dial."

Uncle Bob chuckled nervously. "Now now, let's not get carried away. The last thing I need is more negative media attention. I'm already in hot water with PETA. They think I'm causing Oinky 'undue mental stress' by using him as a mascot." Under his breath, he added, "It's almost like they'd be happier if I turned him into bacon."

Coach Farmer licked his lips. "Oinky does look delicious."

Oinky jumped out of Uncle Bob's arms and scurried into the kitchen. If I were a pig, the kitchen would be the last place I'd go to hide.

Granny must have freaked Uncle Bob out because he nervously said, "Everyone follow me please."

We all followed Uncle Bob into the dining hall. Mom brushed up against Bob and handed him a $5 bill.

"Please sit us as far away from my mother as possible."

Uncle Bob nodded and led us to a table in

the back. My grannies and their pals sat on the other side of the room.

I understood why Mom didn't want to sit next to Granny; it was so she wouldn't embarrass her. But that plan backfired because now Granny hollered across the room.

"Remember to eat some beans, Penny! It helps make you regular! I talked to Dr. Vangingle and he told me all about your colon problems."

Mom put her head in her hands and groaned.

Coach Farmer greedily rubbed his hands together. "Alright gang, let's eat!"

We all jumped up and ran to the buffet. Unfortunately, Granny and her elderly entourage beat us to the punch. Several of the grannies stuck their heads under the sneeze guard to inspect the food, poking it with their canes. A few of the grannies even coughed and sneezed. I made sure to skip those entrees.

We eventually returned to our table with plates full of grub. Mom sighed happily and said, "This is nice."

Shawn, Coach Farmer, and I grunted in response. We were too busy shoveling food down our throats.

"I'm really glad we did this," Mom continued. "It's so touching to see everyone working hard to make the new family work. We're all going to have to make sacrifices, but I think... no, I *know* everything will work out. Especially when we have a new addition to the family."

I gagged on my pop. I hadn't really been paying attention to Mom, mostly because I was keeping an eye out for Chad Michaels and Lily Williams (the poor girl we tricked into seeing Coach Farmer). But I caught that last part.

Mom grabbed my hand. "Are you okay, dear?"

"It depends on what you're talking about. Are you... are you pregnant?"

Mom smiled. "Heavens no. At least, not yet. But Sam and I have talked about... you know, making the union of our two families official."

"Come again?" Shawn sputtered.

With a mouthful of chicken, Coach Farmer garbled, "Penny and I are trying to make a baby."

Coach nudged me in the side and added, "We've been trying *real* hard."

"Gross!" Shawn and I shouted at the same time.

Mom blushed.

"Isn't our family big enough, Mom?" I asked. "Do you really need another freaking kid?"

"Well Harold, your father and I always wanted a large family. Unfortunately, with all of your father's deployments overseas, we never had much time to... you know, have a lot of babies. And I'm not getting any younger. Sam and I talked about it, and we'd really like to give you another brother or sister."

Mom looked up and smiled. "I always did want a baby girl."

Shawn and I exchanged horrified glances. We now realized just how serious things were between our parents. We had to stop the wedding before my mom got pregnant. If that happened, *nothing* would stop Coach from becoming my new 'pappy'.

Shawn pointed toward the door and quietly said, "I think that's him."

I spun around in my chair. A tall, tanned, blond-haired guy just walked through the front door. He was wearing a cut-off t-shirt, jean shorts, and sandals. He looked like he walked right out of an Abercrombie and Fitch billboard.

"Yep, that's Chad alright," I said. "I'll go get him."

"I sure hope this works," Shawn mumbled.

"It's gotta work," I said, glancing at Mom as she and Farmer ate a strand of spaghetti like the two dogs in *The Lady & The Tramp*. When they reached the middle of the spaghetti noodle and started kissing, I just about vomited.

I jumped up and said, "I'll be back, I gotta pee."

Mom and Coach Farmer were still laughing about their silly kiss. They didn't even hear me. I rolled my eyes and hurried over to Chad.

Chad was looking at his reflection in the window, running his fingers through his shaggy hair and flexing his muscles. He didn't notice me until I tugged on his elbow.

"Hiya Chad."

Chad spun around and smiled. "Hey, what's up, bro?" He sounded like a hip surfer from Los Angeles. "What's wrong, you need me to help you find your mom?"

I slapped my forehead. How old did Chad think I was, three?

"Er, no Chad. I'm here to take you to your date. She's my mom."

Chad cocked an eyebrow. "Your mom? Sorry bro, but I think you have me confused with someone else. I'm here to meet this smoking hot lingerie model. Her name's… uh…."

Chad whipped out his phone, I guess to check his email.

"…Penny! Yeah, I'm here to meet this hot

chick named Penny."

I laughed nervously. "That's my mom... a hot lingerie model."

Chad's grin grew wider. I think he thought I was pulling his leg.

"You'll have to do better than that if you wanna trick me. I may look way too cool to be smart, but looks can be deceiving, little bro."

"Oh, I know you're not dumb. You're a pre-med student. You're super smart!"

Chad's smile faded away. "Wait, how did you know that? And how do you know my name?"

"I told you, my mom is your date."

Chad shook his head. "But that's impossible, bro. Penny's online profile said she was 22. How old are you?"

I did some quick math and said, "I'm... six. My mom had me when she was... uh... 16!"

Chad arched his eyebrows. "You look kinda big for a six year old."

"Are you calling me fat?" I snapped.

Chad raised his hands. "No, not at all, bro. I mean, you're kind of husky, but..."

I was about to say something, but I trailed off as one of the most gorgeous girls I'd ever seen walked through the front door. She had long black hair, bright blue eyes, and gleaming white teeth. Her body was bronze and athletic-looking. She wore jean shorts and a red shirt with spaghetti straps. It was Lily Williams, and she looked even more amazing in person than she did online.

Chad muttered, "Wow..."

I turned to find him checking his breath.

"Don't get too excited, Chad. That's not your date."

Chad blew raspberries. "I know, bro, I'm

not... I mean, you know... I mean, man she's hot."

Lily saw us gawking at her and smiled. Chad blushed and turned away. I, on the other hand, stayed cool and walked up to her.

"Hello Lilly."

Lily bent down and said, "Hello little boy. Do you need help finding your mommy?"

"Why does everyone keep asking me that?" I grumbled.

Chad thrust out his hand. "Hi, I'm Chad. You must be from Heaven because you look like an angel."

I burst out laughing. "Oh please, those pickup lines only work in movies."

Much to my surprise, Lily giggled and shook Chad's hand. Sounding like a valley girl, she said, "You're, like, so funny. Let me try now." Lily thought for a moment, then said, "Oh, I got it. So, like, can I have your number, because I, like, forgot mine?"

Chad chuckled. "That's a good one. I never heard that before."

I stared at Chad and Lily in shock. First off, I couldn't believe they liked each other's lame pickup lines. Second off, they both seemed stupider than I thought they'd be. Apparently being a pre-med student doesn't automatically make you smart.

"No, no, no, you guys aren't supposed to like each other," I grumbled. "You're supposed to fall in love with my mom and Coach Farmer."

Lily gave me a puzzled look. "Do what? And how do you know my name? When I came in you, like, said *'Hey Lily'*."

"I'm here to take you to your dates," I said. "Follow me."

I dragged Chad and Lily to our table in the

back. Shawn and Coach Farmer stared at Lily like she was a swimsuit model on the cover of *Sports Illustrated.*

"Hon, what are you doing?" Mom asked.

I started sweating bullets. Now was the moment of truth. I knew Mom wouldn't be happy with what I was about to say, but it was too late to turn back now. I took a deep breath and said, "I'm sorry, Mom, but you're making a terrible mistake. Coach Farmer isn't the right guy for you. Now I know why you agreed to marry him. You're lonely, desperate, and you're afraid no man will accept you because of your webbed feet."

Coach Farmer grabbed Mom's hands and said, "Don't worry, babe. I love your deformed feet. You're like a mutant."

Mom narrowed her eyes. "Harold, can I have a word with you in private?"

Ha, Mom must have thought I was born yesterday. Every kid knows *'Can I have a word with you in private'* is secret code for *'I'm going to smack you with a flyswatter when no one is looking'.* As long as there were witnesses, Mom couldn't lose her temper.

"No, we can talk right here," I said. "Anyway, I know you're desperate, so Shawn and I set up blind dates for you and Coach Farmer."

Coach spit out his meatloaf. "Wait, that hot chick is my date?"

Lily and Mom gasped.

"Smooth, Dad," Shawn muttered.

Chad made a face. "I thought I was seeing some model, not a granny."

Mom crossed her arms. "I am *not* a grandmother, thank you very much. And Harold, you told him I was a model?"

I rubbed the back of my head and murmured, "Among other things."

Lily looked longingly at the door. "I'm sorry, but this is, like, freaking me out. I think I'm gonna go."

"No, wait!" I blurted out. "You should at least stay for dinner. Coach Farmer is buying."

Coach spit out his chocolate pie. "Wait, what?"

Chad grinned at Mom. "I could dig dating an older woman."

"I'm only in my early 30s," Mom growled.

I laughed nervously. "See, everyone's getting along already. Let's eat!"

Chad and Lily uneasily sat down. I asked what they wanted and offered to make their plates. I didn't want to give them a chance to sneak away. By the time I got back with their food, Lily and Coach Farmer were in the middle of an in-depth conversation.

"So you're, like, a particle physicist?" Lily asked.

With a mouthful of baked beans, Coach Farmer mumbled, "I'm a phys-a-what?"

I handed Lily her plate. "Coach is just joking around. He's modest about his intelligence."

"Yeah," Shawn said, helping me out. "My dad's IQ is over 170."

Lily whistled. "Wow, that's, like, high."

Coach smiled. "I didn't know my IQ was so high. I can't wait to tell my third grade teacher. Boy will she feel stupid holding me back twice."

Lily's eyes brightened. "You failed the third grade, too? So did I! We have, like, a lot in common."

I could hear Mom impatiently tapping her

foot under the table.

"So what else did you tell Lily about Sam?" she asked curtly.

"Er, nothing," I said.

"So you're, like, a bodybuilder?" Lily asked.

"Nothing, huh?" Mom growled.

Coach Farmer looked up from his food. "Are you kidding? I haven't worked out in years. I did, however, compete in a few hot dog eating contests in college."

Lily stuck out her tongue. "Ew. That's, like, gross. I'm a vegetarian." She then took a bite of a chicken finger.

Mom struggled not to smirk. "You sure did spend a lot of time vetting our dates, huh?"

"Sadly they were the best of the best," I grumbled. "Here's some good advice: don't look for love online."

"I know, I've already tried," Mom replied.

Chad leaned across the table and grabbed Mom's hands. "So Penny, how about we go do something fun after dinner? We could go to that new club downtown."

Mom yanked back her hands. "I don't know. I've never been clubbing before."

"Oh, I love going clubbing," Lily exclaimed.

Chad grinned. "Really? You wanna go?"

"Sure," Lily said.

"No!" I shouted. Everyone stared at me.

"I mean, you guys are supposed to be dating my mom and Coach Farmer, not each other."

Those words had barely come out of my mouth when Uncle Bob hollered, "What in tarnation do you grannies think you're doing?"

I spun around and watched as Uncle Bob shouted at my grannies and their pals.

"What are you yapping about, Uncle Bob?" Granny snapped.

"I have video cameras all over this restaurant," Uncle Bob said. I looked around and, sure enough, there were several cameras keeping an eye on everyone.

"So what have you been doing, watching me pick my nose?" Granny asked.

"No, I saw you and your pals stuffing food in your purses," Uncle Bob replied.

Granny scoffed. "Why I never! How dare you accuse us of stealing food!"

Almost on cue, Oinky knocked over Granny's purse. Three rolls fell on the floor.

"Aha!" Uncle Bob exclaimed, pointing at the incriminating evidence. "That's stealing! I'm calling the cops."

Mom threw down her napkin. "Oh for crying out loud. This is precisely why I don't like going out in public with my mother. I better step in and say something before she gets herself arrested."

Before Mom could even stand up, Granny hobbled to her feet and shouted, "Run for it, girls! He'll never take us alive!"

Over 30 grannies suddenly jumped up and scurried toward all the exits. They all made sure to grab their purses stuffed with food. Several of the grannies went out the fire exit, causing the alarm to blare and the sprinklers to go off. Within a matter of seconds, everyone in the restaurant was completely soaked. All the other customers ran for the exits as well. Oinky left another present on the floor. Uncle Bob fell to his knees and cried, "Not again!"

Mom, Coach Farmer, Lily, Chad, Shawn and I continued sitting at our table in stunned silence. We were all totally drenched, but no one moved. We were basically in a state of shock.

Chad finally turned to Lily. "So did you wanna check out that new club?"

Lily wiped her face with a napkin. "Sure. Let's, like, get outta here."

Chad and Lily bolted for the door.

Coach Farmer smiled. "I like those guys. If they ever get married, I hope we're invited to the wedding."

Mom glared at me. The mascara running down her face made her look like a witch.

I stretched and said, "Man, what a night. I think we should head home now. It's almost past my bedtime."

Mom turned to Coach Farmer and said, "I'll call you tomorrow, Sam. I'm sorry our date ended in disaster."

Coach shrugged. "It's better than most of the dates I've gone on."

That was sad.

Mom gritted her teeth and snarled, "Good night, Shawn. Luckily for you I'm not your mother yet. Otherwise you'd be in *sooo* much trouble."

Shawn gulped and turned away.

Mom grabbed my ear. "You, however, are a different story."

Mom dragged me out to the car, nearly ripping my ear off in the process.

Chapter Twelve

Tuesday was the day of the Dustin Bopper concert. By then Mom had pretty much forgotten about the disastrous blind date I tried to set her up on. (In our family you learned to repress horrible memories pretty quickly so you could make room for new ones.) But even if Mom hadn't forgotten, I don't think she would have stopped me from going to the concert. It was my first date, and she was thrilled I finally got a girlfriend.

That morning I decided to dress like a combination of April's two favorite things: lame teen pop singers and cheesy vampires. I had Granny fix my hair up like Dustin Bopper's. She put a bunch of hairspray in my hair right after I woke up so I had the whole shaggy bed-hair look going on. It was kind of annoying because my bangs hung over my eyes, but if that's what I had to do to impress April, then I was all for it.

To make myself look like a vampire, I put on a bunch of sunscreen. It made my skin look paler than usual, plus I could tell April sunlight didn't agree with me, just like a real vampire would. I also sucked on a red lollipop so my lips turned bright red. That, of course, would make April think I was drinking blood. To top it all off, I wore a leather jacket and sunglasses.

Even though I dressed up like two things I hated, even I had to admit I looked pretty cool. Unfortunately, all the guys at school *did not* agree.

They all said I looked super hella lame, even my friends. But most of the girls loved my new look. They all ran their fingers through my hair and said I was so dark and mysterious. I'd never been noticed by so many girls before. April even got jealous. She told all the other girls to back off, that I was *her* man. It was seriously the greatest day of my life.

To make sure I wasn't all hot and sweaty during the concert, I pretended to sprain my ankle in gym class. That also got me out of football practice. I went home right after school with Jon. I stayed up in my room and played video games until it was time to pick April up. Mom had to work late, so Granny offered to drive us.

When we got to April's house, I hopped out of the car and hurried up to the front door with a bouquet of flowers I picked from Great Granny's garden. I rang the doorbell and nervously waited for April to answer. Sweat poured from all my pores and my heart started beating like crazy. When April finally opened the door, my heart jumped into my throat. Her hair was pulled back in a ponytail, and she wore a leather jacket and leather pants. She also had on makeup. She looked as beautiful as always, but she also looked like she could kick someone's butt. It was the perfect outfit for a concert.

April held out her arms and spun around. "How do I look?"

"Amazing," I gushed. "You didn't have to dress up just for me."

April giggled. "I didn't do it for you, silly. I did it for Dustin. Hopefully he sees me in the audience and asks me to come up on stage."

I rubbed the back of my head and said, "Er, don't we have nosebleed seats?"

April narrowed her eyes. "Do you really

have to ruin my fantasy?"

I thrust the flowers in April's face before she got too mad. "These are for you."

I expected April to gush about how thoughtful and romantic I was. I never expected her to scream and run around in circles.

"Ahhhh! A bee! Get it away!"

I glanced at the flowers and noticed several bumble bees hovering above them. I threw the bouquet on the ground and shouted, "Go to my granny's car!"

We ran as fast as we could to Granny's mini-van and jumped inside.

"What's going on?" Granny asked.

"We're being attacked by killer bees!" I cried. "Go go go!"

Granny slammed on the gas and tore off down the road. April and I lurched forward and banged our heads against the back of the front seats.

"Put your seatbelts on," Granny ordered. "If I get one more ticket, I lose my license for six months."

We quickly buckled up. I patted April on the back and asked, "Are you alright?"

April looked up. I gasped and jumped back. She looked kind of scary. Her hair was all disheveled, and she had a giant red bump in the middle of her forehead.

"I think I got stung," she groaned. "Do I look okay?"

"Yes," I lied.

Granny pulled onto the highway and cut off an 18-wheeler, causing it to swerve and nearly wreck.

"Slow down, Granny!" I hollered.

Granny responded by going even faster.

"So kids, what's all the fuss with this Dusty Plopper fellow? My pals at the senior center are always griping about how their grandkids listen to him when they visit."

"His name is Dustin Bopper," April said. "And the reason everyone loves him is because he's so amazingly talented and drop-dead gorgeous."

"I still remember my favorite teen pop star," Granny said. "His name was Michael McLovin. Yes-siree bob, Michael McLovin was hot stuff. I bet that Dusty Plopper fella couldn't hold a candle to him."

"His name is Dustin Bopper," April corrected. "And Michael McLovin sucks. My granny likes him, too, and she used to make me listen to his albums."

Granny nearly drove off the road. "What?! Michael McLovin doesn't suck! You take that back!"

"Didn't McLovin go to prison for not paying taxes?" I asked.

Granny snorted. "So? That doesn't mean he wasn't hot stuff back in the day. Besides, every pop star fizzles out after a couple years."

"That won't happen to Dustin Bopper," April said. "He'll be cranking out hits until he's 80."

Granny cackled. "In your dreams, girlie. All you teen girls may worship the ground Buster Pooper walks on right now, but you won't be loving him in a few years when he hits puberty. Pretty soon his voice will start cracking, and zits will pop up out of the woodwork."

April gasped. "None of that will happen to Dustin. He'll stay beautiful and talented forever."

"I really don't feel like arguing with you,"

Granny said. "Let's listen to some McLovin."

Granny put in a CD and turned up the volume. Seconds later, one of McLovin's biggest hits blared from the speakers. Granny bounced around and sang along.

*"Shake that funky booty, shake it pretty girl! Oh shake that funky booty, shake it real good!"*

Granny swerved all over the highway while she danced and sang. Cars slammed on their brakes and honked their horns, but Granny ignored them. It was like she was on another planet.

We got to the arena about ten minutes (and countless near collisions) later. Granny dropped us off in the front and took off. She had a hot date of her own. I felt bad for whoever it was. Granny's dates usually ended in disaster (and a night in jail).

The outside of the arena was packed with trillions of screaming girls. The mob of girls was mixed with bored-looking parents and even more bored-looking boyfriends. A lot of the girls lined up at outside merchandise booths selling Dustin Bopper t-shirts, baseball caps, purses, glowing necklaces, and dolls. The dolls looked just like Bopper. They even had his perfectly coiffed hair. The dolls also had a button on the back that, when pushed, sang a song. It was kind of creepy.

April clutched my hands and jumped up and down like a maniac.

"Omigosh, this is so exciting! Aren't you excited, Harold?"

"This is the greatest day of my life," I mumbled unconvincingly.

April squealed and continued jumping up and down. "Let's go inside!"

I sighed and followed April past security. The guards waved a metal detector over us to make sure we didn't have weapons. If I had thought about it, I would have brought a small blunt object to knock myself out.

"I want to buy a t-shirt," April said, dragging me over to one of the indoor merchandise booths. The lines inside the arena were even longer than the ones outside. We had to wait 20 minutes just to get up to the cashier.

The cashier was a middle-aged woman with glasses and a unibrow. She didn't look thrilled being surrounded by hundreds of hysterical girls.

"Whaddaya want?" the cashier barked.

April breathlessly rattled off, "I want a Dustin Bopper t-shirt, and a Dustin Bopper glow-necklace, and a Dustin Bopper baseball cap, and a Dustin Bopper talking doll."

The cashier arched her unibrow.

"You got the money for that?"

April dug into her purse and pulled out several $20 bills.

"Is this enough?" April asked, placing the money on the counter.

The cashier glanced at the money and said, "You're $20 short."

"What?" I hollered. "This is a scam! You could probably buy all this stuff at Walmart for half the price."

April crossed her arms and pouted, "But I want the stuff now."

She grabbed my hands and fluttered her eyelashes.

"I don't have enough money, Harold. Will you please give me some?"

"Oh alright," I grumbled.

April spun around in a circle and yelped, "Yay!"

I pulled out all the money I had, a $20 bill, and laid it on the counter. Love sure wasn't cheap.

Once April bought all her Dustin Bopper junk, she hurried into the bathroom to change. When she came out, she looked like a walking Dustin Bopper billboard. Dustin's smiling face creepily stared at me from the front of her t-shirt. She had the baseball cap on backwards, just like Dustin always did. Her glow-necklace nearly blinded me. And the Dustin Bopper doll she carried around kept saying cheesy things like *'Love is a battlefield and you're worth fighting for'*, and *'One plus one equals two, and you plus me equals happiness forever'*. Seriously, if I said either of those things to a girl, I'd get slapped so hard my head would spin.

April and I made our way to our seats. The place was completely packed. There were thousands of teen girls crammed into the floor area surrounding the stage. A giant, four-sided television monitor hung from the ceiling so everyone could see the videos and images that went along with the concert. There were three raised sections, and they were all packed as well.

April and I had to climb all the way to the very top of the third raised section. By the time we reached our seats, I was hot, sweaty, and out of breath. The sunscreen I was still wearing began dripping off my face.

"Here we are," I gasped, plopping down in my chair.

April grabbed my hands and gushed, "Thank you so much for coming with me, Harold. This is like the greatest night of my life. It couldn't possibly get any better."

April had no more than said those words when a chubby African-American guy with an eye patch hobbled up the aisle and said, "Hey, you there! You want a front row seat?"

April glanced around and said, "Are you talking to me?"

"No, I'm talking to your lame vampire boyfriend. Yes I'm talking to you!"

April gasped. "Wait, I know you! Sometimes I see you standing next to Dustin Bopper in magazine articles!"

"Yeah, I'm his manager and bodyguard," the one-eyed man said. "Before every show, we look for pretty girls sitting in the nosebleed sections and make their dreams come true by giving them front row tickets."

The man handed April two tickets. "There you go, sweetheart. One for you, and one for Dracula."

"Chicks dig vampires," I said defensively.

"Whatever helps ya sleep at night, kid," Bopper's manager replied.

April screamed, "AHHH! WE GOT FRONT ROW TICKETS!"

I cringed and covered my ears. A few more screams like that and I'd have to borrow Blake's hearing aid.

Bopper's manager led us down to the floor area. We had to weave past thousands of hysterical teen girls waving their arms, tossing beach balls, and basically losing their ever-loving minds. For a young guy like me, it was pretty traumatizing.

The lights suddenly went out, plunging us into complete darkness. The shrieks got even louder. My eardrums vibrated so much, it felt like a tiny midget was inside my head beating on them.

Just when my eyes started to adjust to the darkness, red and green lasers shot out all over the place. After that, bright spotlights swung around the arena. Then the lights came back on and Dustin Bopper floated out of the stage. Soon he was 20 feet in the air.

April dug her nails into my arm. "It's actually him! Isn't he so hot?"

"Uh, yeah, he's gorgeous," I lied.

April squealed even louder.

This was the first time I saw Bopper up close and in person. Usually I just saw his cheesy, smiling face staring at me from countless lockers. For someone so rich, famous, and adored, I couldn't say I was impressed. He looked like a scrawny dork to me. But I kept my thoughts to myself. I definitely didn't want thousands of insane girls clawing my eyes out.

In his soft, girlie voice, Bopper said, "Hello ladies. How are you all doing tonight?"

The crowd responded with a tsunami of ear-splitting screams. Dustin jerked back in mid-air, almost as if a wave of sound washed over him.

"You ready to rock?" he shouted, barely able to be heard over the crowd.

The screaming continued. Dustin started to lower back down to the stage. I noticed about 20 dancers, guitarists, drummers, keyboard players, and other musicians walk out from the back and take their places behind Dustin. I wasn't surprised to see it took so many people to make Bopper sound good.

Once Bopper was back on the ground, he slowly pointed to all the girls in the front row. "This song is for all you pretty little ladies out there."

The backup musicians started playing their

instruments. Shortly after that, Dustin, in a pitch-perfect voice, sang, *"Oh lady, lady, you're so cute... oh lady, lady, let's go smooch!"*

April started crying hysterically, as did all the girls around me. A beach ball bounced off my head and landed on stage. Dustin kicked the ball back into the audience.

I stared at Dustin's mouth. The words I heard didn't match up with what he was saying. It was obvious he was lip-synching.

I tugged on April's sleeve. "Look, the dork's not even singing."

April shoved me. "Quit saying bad things about Dustin. You're just jealous he's so talented."

"What? I'm not jealous! He's not even—ahhh!"

April shoved me into the girl next to me, who immediately shoved me back.

"Shut up! I can't hear!" April went back to waving her arms and crying.

A girl climbed on stage and ran toward Dustin. The one-eyed manager carried her in the back. Dustin didn't even blink. I guess he was used to being mobbed.

I sat there miserably as Dustin continued lip-synching his horrible song. He just kept repeating the same thing over and over again. *"Oh lady, lady, you're so cute, oh lady, lady, let's go smooch!"* Heck, I could do that!

Thankfully, after about five minutes of sounding like a broken record, Dustin (or I should say his recording) stopped. April and the other girls kept on screaming.

Dustin waltzed toward the edge of the stage. "This here is my favorite part of the show. I'm gonna pick one of you pretty ladies and have you come up on stage so I can serenade you with a love song."

My poor ear drums would never recover from the screams that followed.

Dustin glanced at the one-eyed manager. The manager pointed toward April. I gulped as I realized what was happening. The manager didn't give us front row seats out of the goodness of his heart. It was part of the show. More specifically, *April* was about to be part of the show.

Dustin knelt in front of April. April reached up so she could touch his face.

"Hello beautiful," he said.

April screamed and started crying again.

Dustin made a face and stepped back. "Whoa, what's wrong with your forehead?"

April was crying too hard to respond, so I cupped my hand around my mouth and shouted, "She got stung by a bee!"

Dustin nodded and mumbled, "I gotta get someone else besides my blind manager to look for hot girls. These last few haven't been all that."

I think Dustin meant to mumble to himself, but his headset caught some of it. April was too busy crying to hear him. Even with a massive knot on her forehead and makeup running down her face, I still thought she looked beautiful.

Dustin held out his hand. "Come on baby, I wanna sing you a lullaby."

April grabbed his hand and climbed on stage. I crossed my arms and gave Dustin an evil look. He just stole my girlfriend. I didn't have much experience when it came to relationships, but I was pretty sure that was called cheating.

Dustin led April to a chair in the middle of the stage. April put her head in her hands and bawled.

Dustin knelt beside April and soothingly said, "Hey, it's alright. What's your name, sweetheart?"

April lifted her head and sobbed, "April Summers."

"April Summers," Dustin swooned. "That's a pretty name. Who'd you come here with, April?"

April pointed at me and, in between sniffles, blubbered, "My boyfriend Harold."

Dustin looked at me and cracked a smile.

"Harold? What kind of name is that? I didn't know this was 1900."

I felt my cheeks flush. Dustin was lucky my great granny wasn't there. I was named after my great grandpa, and she went off on anyone who made fun of his name.

Dustin stood up and laughed. "Seriously dude, what is up with that outfit? The vampire fad ended a while ago. And not many people can rock my haircut. I hate to be the one to break this to you, but you're definitely not one of them."

The entire arena erupted in laughter. I just stood there and growled.

Dustin turned back to April and grabbed her hand. "You should know this song. It's called *I Grin*."

April squealed and stomped her feet. All the other girls in the arena squealed, too. Unfortunately, I knew all about *I Grin*. It was one of Dustin's biggest, cheesiest hits. Practically every girl at school used it as a ring tone.

Dustin went on to sing the worst song in the history of the world.

*"When you grin, I grin."*

Dustin held his microphone up in the air so

the crowd could sing along. Thousands of voices sang, in unison, *"When you grin, I grin."*

Dustin sang the next verse.

*"When you laugh, I laugh."*

He held up his microphone again and thousands of girls screamed, *"When you laugh, I laugh."*

This continued for the rest of the song.

Dustin: *"When you fall, I fall."*

Thousands of girls: *"When you fall, I fall."*

Dustin: *"When you're sick, I'm sick."*

Thousands of girls: *"When you're sick, I'm sick."*

This went on for ten painful minutes. After Dustin went through all the good and bad things that could ever happen to a person, the song mercifully ended. By now April's makeup was so smeared from all her tears that she looked like a deranged clown.

Bopper made a face when he saw how bad she looked. I saw him mouth to his manager, *"Do I have to?"* The manager nodded and mouthed, *"It's part of the show."*

I didn't realize what was going on until it was too late. Bopper grabbed April's hands, puckered his lips, and gave her a kiss on the cheek.

What happened next was a blur. I wasn't even thinking, it was just pure, raw emotion. I leaped on stage, pointed a quivering finger at Dustin, and shouted, "Get your hands off my girlfriend, you mop-haired freak!"

The one-eyed manager charged toward me, but he was too far away. I lunged toward Bopper and shoved him to the ground.

April jumped on my back and screamed, "Leave Dustin alone! I love him!"

By then the manager got to me. He wrapped his massive arms around my waist and lifted me into the air. I didn't struggle.

The manager whispered in my ear, "Don't tell anyone I said this, but I'm glad you did that. Hopefully you knocked some sense into that boy. He's turning into such a whiny prima donna. The other day he hit me in the eye with a slingshot!"

So that explained the eye patch.

As the one-eyed manager blabbered on about all his problems, I watched the destruction I left behind. Several of Bopper's handlers helped him to his feet. He looked dazed and confused. I laughed when I noticed his 'perfect' hair was now all messy. April was on her knees, crying uncontrollably. All the girls in the audience were crying, too. But I did see some smiling faces, mostly belonging to all the parents and teen boys who were forced to tag along.

April was probably scarred for life, which I kind of felt bad about. She'd probably break up with me first thing Monday morning. But I was also glad I took a shot at Bopper. That was for every teen boy who felt pressured to mimic his stupid hairstyle. I ran my fingers through my hair to mess it up. I also took off my sunglasses and wiped my lips so I didn't look like a vampire. No matter what happened between me and April, I was done being someone I wasn't.

The one-eyed manager plopped me down in the back. Two security guards kept an eye on me while the manager called my mom. As I sat there I thought about how much I would miss dating the hottest girl in school. But I was surprised another girl kept popping up in my mind.

Penelope.

Maybe Coach Heffer was right. Maybe there was something going on between us. Maybe it was time to test the waters.

School was definitely going to be very interesting the following day.

Chapter Thirteen

Mom and Granny picked me up half an hour later. Mom wasn't happy that I knocked down the world's biggest pop star, but Granny thought it was hilarious. It turned out Bopper was so embarrassed at what happened that he decided not to press charges. He didn't want the media constantly talking about how he got 'manhandled' by a 13-year old kid. The cops who were keeping an eye on me backstage let me go with a warning.

On the ride home, I asked if anyone heard from April. Granny said that April's grandmother (one of Granny's bffs) called and said she was picking her up.

"Did she say if April was mad at me?" I asked.

Granny cackled. "Kiddo, I think every girl under the age of 17 is mad at you."

Granny patted me on the head and added, "I'm pretty sure it's over between you two. But don't worry, there are plenty of fish in the sea. Of course, you probably won't find someone as pretty as April. You were lucky she even gave you the time of day. Man, you really blew it."

"Mother, please stop talking," Mom said.

Granny grumbled under her breath and stared out the window.

As soon as we got home, I went straight to bed. But I didn't go to sleep right away because I kept getting texts from kids at school. Apparently my so-called 'attack' on Bopper had made the news, so everyone knew about it. All the guys who texted me said I was a hero. All the girls (except Penelope) said I was scum.

At school the next day, every guy treated me like a king. I was especially shocked when the Dunces grudgingly nodded their approval when we crossed paths in the hall. They hated Dustin Bopper way more than they hated me. All the girls, however, treated me like the worst piece of garbage walking the face of the Earth.

I waited anxiously in English class for April to walk through the door. She finally did just as the bell rang. She still had on her Dustin Bopper t-shirt and glow-necklace.

I mustered up the courage to say, "Hiya April."

"Drop dead, scumbag," April growled as she stormed past.

My heart sank. Granny was right; it was over. I sighed and put my head on my desk. Ms. Meow Meow came up to me and hissed. I hissed back, sending her scurrying to Ms. Hornswaggle.

Lunch wasn't as bad as I thought it would be. Shawn sat with us like he had been, but my friends pretty much left him alone. They were too busy asking details about my brutal beatdown of Dustin Bopper. Of course, I didn't *really* beat him up. I didn't even get to punch him. But by that afternoon the story had evolved to where I apparently took down all of Bopper's bodyguards and ripped his luscious hair off of his pretty-boy head. It was all an exaggeration, but it sure was fun to imagine!

"So Fat-Man, how are things between you and April?" Ben asked.

I nearly spit out my milk. I was hoping no one would ask.

"Didn't you hear her in Ms. Hornswaggle's class?" Abdul asked, chuckling. "She told him to drop dead!"

Penelope glanced over at me. Her lips curled into a rare smile.

"So, uh, you and April are done?"

I returned the smirk. "Yeah, I guess so. 'Drop dead' can't be taken too many different ways."

"No, I guess not." Penelope turned back to Ben and continued talking to him.

My jaw dropped. I expected Penelope to be all excited that April and I broke up, but she seemed indifferent, like she couldn't care less. Even more amazingly, she acted all giddy around Ben. Normally she hated Ben. Something weird was going on, but I didn't know what.

After football practice, Shawn came home with me for another 'study date'. As usual, the house was packed with a bunch of crazy people. Great Granny was in the yard, mowing the grass. (The woman was 85, but she did yard work like she was 20.) The aunts were balled up on the couch, sobbing uncontrollably over another Lifetime movie. (I seriously hated that channel.) Jon and Anthony blasted each other with water guns inside the house. (Poor Betty got soaked.) And Chucky and his pals were rocking out in the basement. Shawn and I hurried up to my room for some peace and quiet.

I sprawled out on my bed and sighed. "Man, what a day."

Shawn collapsed on the floor. "Tell me about it. My arm is so sore."

"Tell your dad he needs to tone down our practices," I said. "We're gonna be so tired by Friday, Buchanan Junior High will run right over us."

"He's not going to listen to me," Shawn said, sitting up. "You should hear him at home. He seriously thinks we're going to blow them out of the water."

"What? That's crazy! We've never blown anyone out of the water!"

"My dad gets carried away sometimes. What can I say?"

Shawn suddenly turned serious. "So hey, I just wanted to say I'm sorry about what happened between you and April. I know you really liked her."

I shrugged. "We broke apart. It happens."

"I don't think that was it," Shawn said. "I think she dumped you because you knocked down Dustin Bop---"

"I know why she dumped me," I snapped. "Do you really need to rub it in?"

"Sorry," Shawn said sheepishly. "So is there any other girl you like? The best way to heal a broken heart is to get back in the dating game."

"Thanks for the advice, Dr. Phil," I replied. "I'm good. I think I need a break from the whole dating scene."

"But you just started dating," Shawn pointed out.

"I'm sorry I haven't had 50 girlfriends like you."

"I've only had three. Seriously though, there's gotta be someone else you like."

"Oh alright, maybe there is someone."

Shawn's eyes got all big, like I was about to

tell him a secret. "Well, who is it?"

My cheeks flushed as I mumbled, "Penelope."

Shawn clutched his stomach and burst out laughing. "Penelope?! You went from liking April Summers to liking Penelope? Hahahaha!"

"What's wrong with Penelope?" I asked defensively.

Shawn's burst of laughter trickled to a few chuckles. "Nothing, I guess. But c'mon, dude. April is like the hottest girl in school, and Penelope is... well, Penelope!"

"What's that supposed to mean?"

"Well, she's not hideous or anything, but... I dunno, she's like a guy in a muscular girl's body. She definitely doesn't act like a lady."

I plopped back down on my bed. "I don't know why I even bother talking to you."

Shawn wiped away his tears. "Alright alright alright, I'm sorry, I got a little carried away. Penelope is... nice."

I could tell Shawn was struggling not to laugh again. "So do you want me to help you snag a date? As you now know from personal experience, my advice is golden."

I sat back up. "Let's quit talking about my love-life for the moment. We have more important things going on."

"Right," Shawn agreed. "Our parents' engagement is getting out of hand, especially now that they're trying to make babies."

We both stuck out our tongues.

"I miss the days when I thought babies came from storks," I muttered. "I'd rather picture that than..."

"ANYWAY," Shawn said, "I think I have a

plan."

"That's what you said about the whole online dating thing, and look how that turned out."

"That was a test run. This is the real deal." Shawn pulled a brochure out of his book bag and tossed it to me.

I opened the brochure and cocked an eyebrow. It was for Emerald Forest, a huge park on the outskirts of town. My dad took me there when I was younger. It had a giant lake, tons of streams, and lots of trails. People liked to camp there.

"What does this have to do with anything?" I asked.

"Remember when you told me your mom hates to go camping? How you used to go all the time with your dad, and your mom never went?"

"Yes," I said, vaguely remembering the conversation. We had actually been talking about a lot of stuff during our 'study dates'. I told stuff to Shawn I didn't even tell my friends, and vice versa. I wouldn't go so far as to say we were friends, but we were definitely former enemies who were beginning to respect and even like each other.

Shawn smirked. "Well, my dad loves to go camping."

It took a few seconds for me to understand what Shawn was getting at.

"You are a freaking genius," I said with a humongous grin.

"I know, right?" Shawn said.

I jiggled my legs, which I always did whenever I got excited about something. "This should work for sure! All you gotta do is tell your dad my mom loves to go camping. If he asks her, she'll feel like she has to go. We can go this Saturday! Nothing's going on that I know of. Then we just have to make sure my mom has a horrible time. She'll freak if she thinks your dad is going to make her go camping every weekend."

"Maybe I can help you guys out."

Shawn and I twirled around and gasped as Granny barged into my room.

"H... how much did you hear?" I stammered.

"Everything, kiddo. I was in the bathroom and heard you through the vents."

I slapped my forehead. I kept forgetting about the vents. I wondered how many times Mom overheard me saying unflattering things about her.

"Don't worry, I ain't gonna rat you out," Granny said, waddling over to my bed. "Quite the contrary. I wanna help."

"Really?" I asked skeptically.

"Yep." Granny plopped down next to me. My bed creaked under all the weight. "I don't know why you're so surprised. I mean, no offense to you, Shawn, but I really don't want two more people moving in here. It's a nut house as it is. And I really don't want your father clogging the shower drain with all his body hair."

"No offense taken," Shawn said. "My dad does have a lot of body hair."

"Actually Granny, you're the one who keeps clogging the drain when you shave your back," I pointed out.

"ANYWAY," Granny said, changing the subject. "I mostly wanna help stop the wedding for *your* sake."

"What do you mean?"

"I know exactly what you're going through. The same thing happened to me when I was younger. After my dad died, my mother tried to remarry. I couldn't stand her fiancé. He wasn't half the man my daddy was. So I stopped the wedding."

"Really?" I said excitedly. "How?"

"Well, my mother's fiancé had a bachelor party the week before the wedding. So I showed up dressed as a dude. When Mother's fiancé said he didn't recognize me, I casually said I was a friend of a friend. He fell for it, which meant I could stand off to the side and secretly take pictures."

"Take pictures of what?" Shawn asked.

"Of Mother's fiancé cheating on her," Granny replied.

"Do what?" I said, confused.

"What I did was bribe a girl to show up at the bachelor party as a dancer," Granny explained. "When she arrived, all the guys got excited and let her in. After she danced a bit, she went over to Mother's fiancé and gave him a kiss. I snapped a couple pics, showed Mother, and voila! No more wedding."

"That's brilliant," Shawn exclaimed.

"Wait a minute," I said. "How old were you when all this happened, Granny?"

Granny rubbed the back of her head and awkwardly replied, "Er, I don't remember. Maybe around your age?"

I crossed my arms. "According to Great Granny, Great Grandpa died about 25 years ago. The math doesn't add up."

"Oh, alright. It was 20 years ago. I was 42."

"Weren't you a little old to be worried about who your mom married?" Shawn asked.

"You don't know me," Granny snapped. "You don't know my life."

I seriously began to think Granny had some major mental issues.

"So do you little brats want my help, or are you gonna keep criticizing me?" Granny asked.

Shawn and I glanced at each other and shrugged.

"Sure, you can help," I said.

"Good. I overheard your camping idea, and I think that's the way to go. This is what we should do."

Granny, Shawn, and I huddled together to discuss our master plan.

## Chapter Fourteen

Friday was the day of our big game against Buchanan Junior High. In my humble opinion, we did a pretty good job. We only lost 35-10. Thankfully, that was the second-to-last game of the season. We were probably the only football team in the country that actually looked forward to the end of the season. This time Coach didn't cry after we lost. I think he finally accepted that we totally sucked.

Saturday was our big camping trip. Things turned out just as I hoped they would. Shawn told Coach Farmer that my mom and I loved to go camping, but we hadn't been since my dad died. Coach Farmer called my mom and said he wanted to take the whole family camping, even Betty and the aunts. Mom pretended to be excited and said yes. We were good to go!

That morning we loaded up Granny's minivan and Coach Farmer's pickup truck. Even though I hadn't gone camping in four years, I still had all of my dad's stuff. And of course Coach Farmer had a bunch of camping gear, too. We packed cool clothes for the hot afternoon, and warm sweaters and jackets for the cool nights. We also brought along tents, sleeping bags, and coolers loaded with pop, hot dogs, lunchmeat, marshmallows, and other snacks. After everyone slathered on sunscreen, we hopped into the cars.

Mom, the grannies, the aunts, Jon, Anthony, Chucky, and Betty Beagle crammed into the minivan. Shawn, Coach Farmer, and I hopped into Coach's pickup truck. We then took off for Emerald Forest.

Along the way, Coach Farmer put in a few of his classic rock CDs. We listened to The Doors, KISS, and Guns N Roses. I knew all the classics because my dad used to listen to that stuff (who listened to it with his dad). It was actually kind of a fun ride.

After half an hour of driving, we finally got into the country. Coach let down his window so we could breathe in the fresh country air. There was nothing to see for miles but deep blue skies dotted with white fluffy clouds, rolling green hills, and patches of trees. It made me miss my dad more than ever.

Soon we were on the outer edges of Emerald Forest. I could tell because more and more trees popped up. Coach Farmer inhaled deeply and sighed. It wasn't an irritated sigh, either. It was like he was happy and content.

Coach reached over and patted me and Shawn on our heads. "I'm so glad we're doing this. I always envisioned having a big, happy family, and going on giant family vacations and camping trips. We're gonna have a lot of fun over the coming years."

Shawn and I glanced at each other and frowned. Comments like that *almost* made me feel bad for what we were about to do.

Pretty soon shadows swallowed us up, even though it was still sunny out. We had officially entered Emerald Forest. Dozens of treetops hung over us, blocking out the sun. The soft buzzing sound of thousands of insects danced on my eardrums. I knew Mom and the aunts were freaking out right about now. They hated bugs.

A line of traffic crawled through the main entrance of the park. A crisply dressed park ranger sat in his booth and waved people through. We eventually found an awesome spot in a meadow surrounded by trees. The lake was only a few hundred yards away. A boat rental place was nearby, too.

Once we parked, we began unloading our stuff. We set up our tents around a burned-out campfire in the middle of the meadow. Next to the campfire was a charcoal grill.

Coach came over to me and Shawn and said, "Why don't you boys go gather up some firewood for the campfire?" He handed us giant garbage bags to put the wood in.

"I'll help," Granny said, waddling over.

"That's okay, Granny, we got it," I said.

Granny pinched the back of my neck and loudly whispered, "I need to go with you. It's all part of the plan."

Coach Farmer scratched his head. "What plan?"

Shawn chuckled nervously. "Er, nothing, Dad. You're hearing things again. We'll be back in a bit."

Shawn shoved me and Granny into the forest. "Smooth, guys," he grumbled.

"I can't help it my granny doesn't know how to whisper," I griped.

Once we were deep in the woods and well out of hearing range, I said, "So what's up, Granny? Why'd you tag along?"

"Because, doofus, I need to make sure you

get the right kind of firewood."

I picked up a thick, solid log and said, "Like this?"

"Nope." Granny dug through the brush and picked up a rotted, termite-infested log crawling with all sorts of bugs. "Like this."

Shawn and I jumped back in horror.

"That's gross!" I cried. "Put it down before the bugs get on us!"

"You dingbats aren't thinking clearly," Granny said, still clutching the bug-covered log. She didn't seem to notice or care that the bugs were crawling up her arm. "We're trying to make sure Penny has a terrible time, right?"

"Right," I said.

"Well, what's the one thing that always ruins a picnic?"

Shawn and I shrugged.

"Ants," Granny cackled, shaking her rotted log in the air. Dozens of insects flew in our faces. Shawn and I screamed like little girls and jumped back again.

Granny tossed the log into her garbage bag. "What we'll do is grab a couple more of these bug-infested logs. When we get back, I'll drop a few around the perimeter of our campsite. I'll also toss one or two of the logs into Penny's and Sam's tent. By tonight, bugs will be crawling everywhere, especially after I sprinkle around this bag of sugar."

Granny whipped a bag of sugar out of her pocket and waved it in the air.

"You are like some sort of evil genius," I said, impressed.

"I'm glad you're on our side," Shawn added.

We spent the next 20 minutes gathering up firewood. Whenever we found a good log, we tossed it into our bags. When we found nasty termite-infested logs, we threw them into Granny's bag. Once the bags were full, we headed back to camp.

Everyone was still in the middle of unpacking, so Granny and I discreetly tossed several of the termite-infested logs into Mom's tent. Granny also emptied her bag of sugar.

"Hehehe, I can't wait to hear Penny's shrieks of terror when she climbs into her sleeping bag," Granny chortled. "She hates bugs."

"Not as much as the aunts," I said, pointing to Aunt Kathy and Aunt Patty. They were both wearing black garbage bags like they were ponchos. They also put pantyhose over their heads. They were basically wearing a poor-man's bug suit.

"Why are there so many bugs flying around?" Aunt Patty cried, waving her hands in the air.

"Um, maybe cuz we're outside?" Chucky said.

"Here Sissy, use some bug spray." Mom tossed the bottle of spray to Aunt Patty.

Aunt Patty pressed down on the bottle's trigger, but nothing came out.

"Oh no, Sissy! The bug spray's empty!"

"We're all gonna die!" Aunt Kathy cried, running around in circles.

Granny wobbled over and snickered. I cocked an eyebrow and asked, "Did you have something to do with the empty bug spray bottle, Granny?"

"Maybe," Granny cackled. "Now everyone will get tons of bug bites, increasing the horribleness of this camping trip."

"That's great, Granny. There's just one

problem: now *we're* going to get bit!"

Granny stopped laughing. "Dang, you're right. I didn't think about that."

A mosquito suddenly bit my arm. I flicked it away, but the damage was already done. That was the first of what was sure to be many bites.

"This is going to be a long night," I grumbled.

Coach Farmer clapped his hands. "Let's not let a lack of bug spray affect our afternoon. How about we go fishing? We can rent a couple boats and go out on the lake!"

"I don't know, Sam. I'm not a good swimmer," Mom said nervously. "What if I fall overboard?"

Coach scoffed. "Don't be ridiculous, honey. It's not like a giant wave is going to wash over us. It's a quiet, tranquil lake. Plus, the boats have life preservers."

"Oh alright," Mom said reluctantly.

We all gathered up our fishing rods and fake bait and walked down to the boat rental place. The boats were pretty big, so we only needed two.

Mom, Coach Farmer, Granny, Great Granny, Shawn, and I got in one boat. The aunts, Chucky, Jon, Anthony, and Betty Beagle got in the other one. Once we were strapped in our life preservers, we paddled out to the middle of the lake.

Granny wasn't paying attention when she flipped back her fishing rod, so her hook caught on Coach Farmer's hat. When she whipped the fishing pole forward, Coach's hat went flying out into the middle of the lake.

"Oh no, that's my lucky hat!" Coach cried.

Mom patted Coach on his bald head. "Oh dear, you better put some sunscreen on your head before you get sunburned."

Coach scoffed. "What are you talking about? My hair will protect my scalp from harmful solar radiation."

"What hair?" Granny hollered.

Mom rummaged around in her purse and muttered, "I could have sworn I put the sunscreen in here. Where on Earth could it have gone?

Granny nudged me in the side yet again. "Guess who hid the sunscreen?"

"Jeez Granny, it almost seems like you want to stop this wedding more than I do," I whispered. "So where did you put it?"

"I tossed it in the woods," she replied casually.

"WHAT?" I hollered. "Now we're all going to burn!"

"Hmm, I didn't think about that," Granny muttered.

Apparently she didn't think about a lot of things.

I flung out my line and waited for a nibble. We all sat out in the middle of Emerald Lake for about an hour. No one caught a single fish. The only interesting thing that happened was a dragonfly landed on Aunt Patty's pantyhose-covered face. She and Aunty Kathy screamed bloody murder for nearly ten minutes. Oh, and Betty pooped in their boat. They screamed about that, too. Other than that, it was a pretty uneventful fishing trip. That was, until Coach Farmer's line went taut.

Coach jumped up so excitedly he rocked the boat. "Holy mackerel, I caught something!"

"Maybe it's a mackerel," Granny cracked.

Coach tried to reel it in, but he had trouble. With sweat pouring down his bright red face, he mumbled, "Hooboy, this is a big one. Maybe it's a shark."

"Don't be stupid, there aren't any sharks in Emerald Forest," Granny said. "It's probably a whale."

"Someone help!" Coach cried. "I'm losing my grip!"

Granny wobbled over and grabbed Coach's fishing rod. "Pull, you big oaf! Pull!"

Granny and Coach yanked back on the rod as hard as they could, but nothing plopped into the boat. Whatever Coach caught was freaking huge!

That's when the most brilliant idea in history popped into my head. I pretended I had a catch and hollered, "Mom, help!"

Shawn grabbed my rod. "I'm right here, dork. I'll help."

"No!" I shouted, stomping on Shawn's toes. Shawn yelped and hopped around on one foot.

"Er, I mean, I want Mom to help me," I said.

Mom hurried over. "What's wrong, dear? Do you have a catch, too?"

"Yes! Grab my pole and pull back as hard as you can. It's about to drag me overboard!"

Mom grabbed my rod and yanked it up in the air, just like I hoped she would. I immediately let go, causing Mom to topple out of the boat and into the lake. There was a loud splash, followed by a small wave of water crashing into the boat.

"Holy mackerel!" Coach Farmer cried, letting go of his rod. "Penny, are you okay?"

Mom flapped her arms. "I can't swim! I can't swim!"

"Don't worry, babe, you're wearing a life preserver," Coach hollered back.

That did nothing to calm Mom down. If

anything, she got *more* hysterical.

I glanced at the other boat. Jon and the aunts were crying uncontrollably. I guess they really thought Mom was going to drown.

Granny thrust one of our paddles into Mom's face. "Grab the oar, honey!"

Mom stopped splashing around and grabbed the paddle. Granny, Great Granny, and Coach pulled back as hard as they could, yanking Mom into the boat. She was completely soaked, but other than that she seemed okay.

Coach grabbed his fishing rod and, with Granny's and Great Granny's help, finally hauled his catch out of the water. It turned out to be a tire.

"Dagnabit," Coach grumbled.

We quickly paddled back to shore so Mom could change into warm clothes. At least, that was the plan. But Mom went through her entire bag and couldn't find anything.

"What happened to all my stuff?" Mom cried.

"Oh no, Sissy, my stuff is missing, too." Aunt Patty held up her empty bag.

"So's mine," Chucky said.

"We're been robbed!" Aunt Kathy bawled.

It turned out all of our clothes were gone. Everyone was upset except for Granny, who stood off to the side grinning like some sort of demented clown.

"Are you behind the missing clothes?" I asked her in a hushed whisper.

"Of course," Granny said. "While everyone was putting up the tents, I snatched all the clothes and tossed them deep in the woods. It's gonna get quite cool tonight, and we're all wearing shorts and t-shirts. Penny will have a miserable night for sure, especially now that she's soaking wet. That was a nice touch by the way, pretending to have a bite. I'll have to use that the next time Mother and I go fishing."

"I want my mom to break up with Coach Farmer, not die of hypothermia," I said.

Granny flapped her wrist. "Don't be such a drama queen. She'll be fine."

We glanced at Mom, who was sitting on a rock, shivering uncontrollably.

"Or not," Granny mumbled.

Aunt Patty did her best to dry Mom off with a towel. "Maybe we should go home, Sissy. You're soaked."

Coach Farmer lowered his head and sighed. "Your sister's right, Penny. We should probably get outta here. This trip has been a bust."

"Wait!" I shouted.

Everyone stared at me.

"I don't think Mom wants to leave just yet," I said. "How are we all going to live together if we can't handle a little camping trip?"

Shivering, Mom said, "H... H... Harold is r... r... right. I'll be f... f... fine."

The aunts didn't look thrilled, but Coach Farmer was all smiles.

"You won't regret this, Penny," he said gleefully. "We're gonna have a grand ole' time. Just you watch."

"How about we make something to eat?" I suggested.

Coach slapped me on the back so hard, I nearly fell face-first into the burned-out campfire. "Great idea, son. I'll get the grill going."

While Coach warmed up the charcoal, Shawn and I started the next phase of our plan. We set out an empty pitcher, poured in a cup of lemonade mix, sprinkled in some sugar, emptied a few bottles of water, and added our secret ingredient: a liquid laxative.

While stirring our 'colon-cleansing' drink, I snickered and said, "This should make everyone miserable for sure."

Shawn chuckled, too. "Yeah, everyone but us. I'll make us something else."

Shawn grabbed another pitcher and made blue Kool-Aid, minus the laxative.

"Make sure you hide the Kool-Aid when you're done," I said. "Otherwise, Mom might drink that instead."

Shawn sat the Kool-Aid inside one of our coolers. Once Coach Farmer finished grilling up some hotdogs, we sat down at a couple picnic tables and dived into our camping feast. I was pleased to see almost everyone pour themselves a cup of lemonade (except me and Shawn, of course). Even Granny gulped down a couple glasses. I forgot to warn her about the 'special ingredient'. She was *sooo* going to kill me.

"Mmmm, this lemonade is really good," Aunt Kathy said. "There's something different about it."

Aunt Patty smacked her lips. "I agree, Sissy. I can't quite place my finger on it, but it's almost like there's a special ingredient."

Mom turned to me and asked, "What are you drinking, dear?"

"Blue Kool-Aid," I replied, trying to stay cool. "Shawn and I didn't feel like drinking lemonade."

"Yeah, lemonade hurts my stomach and makes me have to poo," Shawn said.

I covered my mouth to hide my chuckles.

Granny grabbed the lemonade pitcher and poured another cup. "I think you're both crazy. The lemonade is absolutely deli…"

Granny was interrupted by a thunderous fart.

Great Granny blushed. "Oops! My bad, everyone. I tooted. That hasn't happened since Watergate. I don't know what came over me."

"Mother, that was foul," Granny hollered. "If I did that you'd…"

Granny was cut off by yet another fart. This time she blushed.

"Oops! That was me."

Chucky sniffed the air and frowned. "Yuck. What's that smell?"

Granny slowly stood up and stepped back from the table. The horrible stench that smelled like death seemed to be coming from her backside.

Granny touched her butt and gasped. "Holy crud, I just pooped my pants!"

Jon and Anthony laughed and clapped like they were watching some kids' comedy show. The rest of the family looked horrified.

"I told you to lay off the prunes," Aunt Kathy said. "They cause you to…"

Another fart erupted out of someone's rear end.

Aunt Patty jumped up and said, "Oh dear, I need to poot. Where's the bathroom?"

"There is no bathroom," Coach Farmer said. "We're in the woods."

Aunt Patty clutched her stomach and groaned. "Ohhh, I really have to go."

"Oh no, what's Sissy gonna do?" Aunt Kathy wailed. She suddenly clutched her stomach and groaned. "Wait, what am I gonna do? I gotta go now, too!"

By now almost everyone was on their feet, dancing around in circles. Every few seconds a deafening fart would rip through the campsite, sending birds fleeing to safety.

The only people who stayed put were me, Shawn, and Jon. I glanced at Jon's cup. He was drinking blue Kool-Aid, too. He made a wise choice.

"Okay everyone, don't panic," Coach Farmer grunted, his face as red as a tomato. "We'll just do what our ancestors did back in the olden days: go in the bushes."

Granny looked like she was doing the hokey pokey. "What?! That's nasty! What are we supposed to use for toilet paper?"

"What do you think?" Coach Farmer hollered, wiggling his leg. "Leaves!"

Betty Beagle ran back and forth, barking at my dancing, jiggling family. I think she thought they were playing around. The whole thing was pretty hilarious to watch.

Granny flapped her arms so hard I was afraid she'd take off. "I can't hold it any longer! I gotta go!"

Granny dove into the bushes. A bunch of terrified squirrels, chipmunks, and raccoons ran out of the bushes and scampered up the trees. I couldn't blame them. If I saw Granny taking a dump, I'd probably climb a tree, too.

The rest of the lemonade drinkers followed Granny's lead. Mom, Coach Farmer, the aunts, Great Granny, Chucky, and little Anthony leaped into the bushes to let nature do its thing. Pretty soon the entire campsite reeked like an outhouse.

Holding my nose, I said, "Maybe this wasn't such a good idea."

"Of course it was," Shawn replied in a nasally voice. He was holding his nose, too. "The wedding is definitely off now."

Jon gulped down the rest of his Kool-Aid and smacked his lips. "Mmmm! That was good!

I drunk the rest of mine and said, "I agree. It tastes a little different than it usually does, but I like it."

"That's because I added your 'special ingredient'," Jon replied casually.

I cocked an eyebrow. "Do what?"

Watching a butterfly float above his head, Jon said, "I was watching you from the bushes when you made the lemonade. I saw you pour something in it, but you didn't put it in the Kool-Aid. I figured you forgot, so I put it in when you weren't paying attention."

I felt my face turn pale. Shawn's face looked pretty white, too.

I gulped and said, "You mean... you put the laxative in the..."

A weird gurgling nose erupted from the pit of my stomach, like an atomic bomb going off inside my body. I felt something race through my intestines and shoot straight for my...

"Oh wow!" I cried, leaping to my feet. "That laxative's no joke!"

Shawn jumped up a split-second later. "You're not kidding! Usually your mom's cooking is the only thing that makes me go this quickly."

"What's a lack-a-duck?" Jon asked.

"You'll find out in a few seconds," Shawn grunted, dashing for the bushes. I followed after him, with Jon close behind.

Chapter Fifteen

We stayed in the bushes for an hour. That's about how long it took the laxative to work its magic. By the time we were done, we were all hot, sweaty, smelly, and exhausted. And our campsite totally reeked. Even Betty seemed disgusted, and she ate her own poop! Mom was so exhausted that she went straight to her tent. She ran out screaming two seconds later.

"Okay, that's it, let's go home!" Mom hollered, shaking bugs out of her hair.

I had hoped our horrible camping trip would be enough to make Mom rethink the wedding. But by the time we got home, Mom and Coach were laughing about the whole experience.

"What a terrible night," Mom giggled as we brought our camping gear into the house. "But you know what? It's a story we'll probably be telling friends and family for years to come."

"So you're not mad about the horrible time we had?" I stammered.

"Well, I can't say I'm thrilled, but..."

Mom looked over at Coach Farmer and grinned. "If I'm going to have crazy times like this, there's no one I'd rather spend them with than Sam."

My mouth fell open in shock. All my hard work, all my explosive diarrhea and bug bites and sunburned skin, had been for nothing. The camping trip from Hell didn't tear Mom and Coach Farmer apart. It brought them closer together!

Shawn and I looked at each other and frowned. Our parents were much tougher opponents than we ever imagined. I was so upset, I went straight to bed.

I slept until 2:00 the following afternoon. Since it was a Sunday, I pretty much had the whole day to do whatever I wanted. Unfortunately, Shawn thought it would be a good idea if a few of us got together and practiced some plays for our game against Nixon Academy. We called up Abdul, Ben, Blake, Penelope, and a couple others. Everyone but Blake and Abdul were busy. I was kind of surprised Ben and Penelope didn't want to come, but I brushed it off.

We decided to go to this little park behind my old stomping grounds, William Henry Harrison Elementary School. What was cool about the park was that it had a grassy football field. Chucky was going to the park to play basketball, so he offered to take us with him.

We got to the park around 4:00. It was pretty crowded, but there was no one on the field. Blake, Abdul, and I took up offensive line positions and walked through a bunch of plays. Shawn corrected us whenever we made a mistake. Shawn may have gotten on my nerves from time to time, but the guy was a genius when it came to football.

Shawn also worked on his passes. He had me and Blake run some tight end and wide receiver routes. We didn't catch a single pass, though. It wasn't Shawn's fault, we just sucked. There was a reason we were linemen and not receivers.

After about an hour of running plays, we took a break. It was a cool day, but I was still hot and sweaty from all the running Shawn made us do.

I dumped half my water bottle over my head and shook like Betty did after getting a bath.

I plopped down on a bench and said, "I wonder why Penelope and Ben couldn't make it? Penelope always wants to practice."

Blake loudly replied, "All I know is that Ben and Penelope have been spending a lot of time together recently."

I spit out my water. "Do what?"

Abdul nudged Blake in his stomach, causing him to shut up. I got the sinking feeling they knew something I didn't. I hadn't even realized Ben and Penelope were hanging out on their own because I was so focused on stopping my mom's wedding. I'd have to keep an eye on those two.

We had just walked back out on the field when a familiar voice cackled, "Well look who it is, boys. Dumb, dumber, dumberer, and dumbest."

My pals and I twirled around and scowled as Jasper, Cletus, and Rufus marched toward us. Jasper had a football in his hand. Apparently they had the same plan we did.

"Leave us alone, Dunce," I said.

Jasper got up in my face. "Hey, it's a free country. I can go wherever I please."

"Just go away, Jasper," Shawn grumbled. "We're not bothering you."

Jasper turned to Shawn and smiled. "Well well well, if it isn't the traitor himself."

Jasper shoved Shawn in the chest, causing him to stagger back and nearly fall over. Rufus and Cletus clapped and giggled like psychotic, Ritalin-deprived 5-year olds. Abdul and Blake backed away. They hated confrontations. I, however, stood my ground.

"Leave him alone, Dunces!"

Jasper stared at me with a combination of admiration and pity. "What an interesting turn of events. The biggest nerd in school sticking up for the bully who used to pick on him. You must either be stupid or have a terrible memory."

"I'm not stupid, and I *definitely* haven't forgotten all the mean things Shawn's done to me. But right now we have a bigger enemy: *you*."

I shoved Jasper in the chest. I must have caught him off guard because he toppled to the ground.

Rufus and Cletus gasped, shocked their leader was knocked flat on his back. For the first time *ever,* cracks began to appear in the Dunce Wall.

Jasper slowly got to his feet. "You just made the biggest mistake of your life, punk."

"I'm not scared of you." I'm sure my quivering voice gave me away.

Jasper cracked his knuckles. "Oh really? Well, you should be. You don't stand a chance going up against me alone. Do you really think your friends are gonna help you?"

I glanced at Blake and Abdul. They stood about 20 feet away, shaking in their boots.

Abdul stammered, "C... c... can't we all just g... g... get along?"

"Shut up, you filthy terrorist," Jasper snapped. "Go back to Iraq."

Abdul narrowed his eyes. "I'm an American, jerk. I was born here. And my parents are from Pakistan, not Iraq."

"Yeah, quit making fun of my best friend," Blake said.

Jasper scoffed. "Aren't you Jewish, 'Bionic

Man'? I thought all Jews and Muslims hated each other."

"Just because some Jews and Muslims fight with each other doesn't mean we have to," Abdul replied. It was probably one of the smartest and most eloquent things he ever said.

Jasper glanced around and frowned. "Where's your scrawny Japanese friend? He has a smart mouth. I was hoping to pound his face in."

"Ben's Chinese, idiot, and he's not here," I growled.

Jasper scoffed again. "Chinese, Japanese, they all look the same."

An evil grin crept across Jasper's face. "And where's your Mexican girlfriend? I know some of her family members are here illegally. Maybe I'll call up immigration."

I felt my ears turn red. "Penelope's not my girlfriend! We're just fri---"

I trailed off as my brain processed the second half of Jasper's comment.

"Wait, what?"

Jasper sneered. "You heard me. Maybe I'll call immigration and have your girlfriend's family deported back to Mexico."

"You stupid---"

I took a swing at Jasper's face, which turned out to be a horrible mistake. Jasper clutched my fist with his right hand before I could smash it into his nose. Sharp stabs of pain shot up and down my arm. I cried out and fell to my knees, but Jasper didn't let go. He towered over me, still clutching my hand and twisting my arm.

"You can at least make this interesting and put up a fight," Jasper taunted.

"Let him go!" Shawn lunged toward Jasper,

but Rufus and Cletus pinned him to the ground.

"Say I'm the best and you suck," Jasper ordered.

"You're the best and I suck!" I wailed, blinking back tears. "Just let me go!"

"No," Jasper said, squeezing even harder. Every bone in my hand felt like they were about to crumble.

Just when I thought I was going to black out, someone shouted, "Leave him alone!"

I was in too much pain to see what was going on, but I did notice a flurry of movement. Jasper let go of my hand, causing most of my pain to evaporate. I spun around and watched as Uncle Chucky towered over Jasper, who was sprawled out on the ground.

Chucky's hair was pulled back in a ponytail. He still had on his dark shades, but his shirt was off. Jasper's eyes bulged at the sight of Chucky's six-pack abs and slender, muscular body. He looked like a model that could totally kick someone's butt. I'm sure the 'kick butt' part was running through Jasper's mind.

Chucky turned to me and asked, "Are you okay?"

I shook my throbbing hand and grunted, "Yeah. I don't think anything's broken."

Jasper slowly got off the ground. "I know you. You're Harold's gay uncle. My older brother goes to high school with you. He makes fun of you all the time."

Since Chucky always wore his sunglasses, I could never tell from his eyes what he was thinking. I usually had to look for facial clues. But this time his mouth was a tight line, revealing no emotion whatsoever. He did clench his fists, though.

"I know your brother," he replied coolly.

Jasper chuckled. "I hope so. From what I hear, he picks on you pretty good."

I was shocked. I thought Chucky never got picked on. He was so cool!

Chucky was about to say something, but then he scoffed and waved Jasper off.

"You're not worth it, dude." He turned to me and asked, "You ready to go?"

"Yeah," I grumbled, grabbing our ball. I really wanted to pound Jasper's face in, but he proved I was no match for him. Chucky could totally whoop up on him if he wanted to, but he liked to avoid fights at all cost. Chucky was like one of those anti-war, 'give peace a chance' hippies.

We had just started walking to the car when Jasper said, "Look boys, the gay guy and his boyfriends are running away with their tails between their legs."

Chucky stopped dead in his tracks, causing me to nearly bump into him. He turned and stared at Jasper. His face was still emotionless, but his cheeks turned fiery red.

Jasper grinned. "Ohhh, looks like I touched a nerve."

"Duh, maybe we should leave them alone, Jasper," Cletus said.

"Yeah," Rufus agreed. "They're running away. What more do you want?"

It was nice to see Rufus and Cletus had limits when it came to their bullying ways. Jasper, however, had no limits.

"My daddy says it's not natural for boys to like boys," Jasper snarled. "But I didn't need him to tell me that, I already knew."

I lunged toward Jasper, but Chucky held me

back.

"No Harold," he said forcefully. "Don't succumb to his level. It's what he wants."

I took a quivering deep breath and started to walk away. That's when Jasper shouted some of the most vile, disgusting, hate-filled gay taunts I ever heard. I twirled around, screamed, and tackled Jasper to the ground.

Chucky and Shawn immediately pulled me off of Jasper and dragged me to the car. Cletus and Rufus gawked at me in wide-eyed wonder while their leader remained flat on his back, sprawled out like roadkill.

Once we were in the car, my friends jumped around in excitement.

"Oh my gosh, that was amazing!" Abdul gushed. "You destroyed Jasper!"

"I know, he was totally shocked!" Shawn said giddily.

My friends kept going on and on about how awesome I was, but Chucky was oddly quiet. After Chucky dropped my friends off, we drove the rest of the way home in complete silence. I opened my mouth several times to say something, but nothing came out. I usually never had trouble striking up a conversation with Chucky. But this was different. I wasn't sure if he was mad, sad, happy, or indifferent. If only he'd take off his sunglasses. Then I'd have an easier time reading him.

Chucky finally pulled into our driveway. I gulped when I saw Mom's car. She'd freak if she found out I got into a fight.

Chucky took his keys out of the ignition and sighed. I twiddled my thumbs, waiting for him to say something.

"I wish you didn't tackle that boy," he

finally said.

"But Chucky, you heard what he said! I wasn't going to stand there and..."

Chucky raised his hand, cutting me off. "Hang on, man, let me finish. I usually don't condone violence, but..."

Chucky flashed me a devilish grin. "...deep down inside, I'm glad you tackled Jasper."

I returned the smile. "Really?"

"Yeah, man. No one ever sticks up for me. Everyone thinks gay slurs don't bother me because I act like they don't. But really they do."

"Gee, I didn't think anything bothered you. You're always so calm and relaxed."

"Yeah, well, it's all an act."

For the first time since I could remember, Chucky took off his shades. I was shocked by what I saw. Chucky's eyes were red and moist, like he had been fighting back tears. I had never seen Chucky cry before. *Ever.*

"This is why I always wear sunglasses," Chucky said, wiping his eyes. "I don't want people to know their taunts bother me. I figured if bullies don't see me upset, then they'll leave me alone, that I'm not worth their time. It usually works, but not always. Jasper's brother taunts me all the time. I do my best to ignore him, but sometimes it's hard."

"I'm sorry, Chucky," I replied quietly. "I had no idea."

"Don't worry about it, man," Chucky replied. "I'm a big boy, I can take care of myself. But hopefully now you realize *everyone* gets bullied about something. I get picked on because I'm gay. You get picked on because of your weight. Shawn probably gets picked on for being the principal's son. I'm sure Penelope gets bullied for being a

Hispanic tomboy, Blake gets picked on for his hearing aid and being Jewish, Ben gets bullied for being a scrawny Asian kid, and Abdul gets taunted for being Muslim. I bet even the Dunces get bullied. After all, you pretty much just kicked Jasper's butt. Technically *you* were the bully, at least for a moment."

"That's not true," I protested. "You can't... I mean, I didn't... I mean..."

I trailed off as I pondered Chucky's words. Maybe he had a point.

"There's a fine line between being a bully and being a victim," Chucky said quietly. "I'm a fierce advocate for sticking up for yourself, but you have to make sure you don't overreact. Otherwise you risk becoming the very thing you hate."

"What am I supposed to do then? Just ignore them? Let them say and do whatever they want?"

Chucky sighed again. I don't think he was irritated with me, I think it was the situation. "No. You just need to realize there will always be bullies, even when you grow up. Bullying continues into adulthood. In some ways it becomes worse. You have to put up with mean bosses, mean coworkers, mean family members. Sometimes you have to deal with cruel leaders and politicians, dictators and kings.... Those are the scariest bullies of all... the world leaders. The biggest difference between kid bullies and adult bullies is that adult bullies can start wars."

"So what should I do the next time someone picks on me or my friends?" I asked. "What should I do when someone picks on *you*?"

Chucky looked out his window. "You should always stick up for yourself, for your friends, family, and loved ones. But you can't start brawling every time someone says something you don't like. Otherwise, you'll always be at war. Sometimes you can defeat a bully just by ignoring their taunts. Bullies crave attention. If you take that away from them, you take away their reasons for bullying you in the first place. "

That wasn't really the answer I wanted. I wanted Chucky to tell me it was okay to punch someone like Jasper in the face, then run like mad. (I definitely wouldn't wait around for Jasper to punch back.)

"I guess you're right," I grumbled.

Chucky rustled my hair. "You're a good, smart kid. Middle school is tough. Trust me, I know. But you'll get through it. Just remember to always straddle that fine line between standing up for yourself and starting an endless feud. If you do that, you'll be alright."

I nodded. Chucky really was one of the smartest people I knew. Plus, the fact that Chucky got picked on made me realize just how stupid bullies were. If they picked on someone as cool as Chucky, then their opinions meant nothing. I no longer feared them, I pitied them. Maybe I would try and ignore the Dunces. It's not like they had a lot of support at school nowadays. If everyone ignored them, maybe they would fade away.

Chucky and I got out of the car and walked toward the house.

"Hey, Chucky? Do you think we can maybe not mention what happened to my mom? She'll freak out if she hears I got into a fight."

"What fight?" Chucky said with a smirk.

Chucky hugged me as we walked through the front door.

## Chapter Sixteen

At lunch the next day, Abdul and Blake rambled on about how I destroyed Jasper. Shawn was still in the lunch line, so he wasn't there to back them up. Still, Penelope and Ben seemed to believe them, especially when they pointed out Jasper's black eye.

"No way!" Penelope squealed. "That's so awesome!"

"Thanks," I said sheepishly. "So how come you and Ben couldn't make it yesterday? I could have used your help manhandling the Dunces."

"Well, Fat-Man, Penelope and I...," Ben started to say.

Penelope cut him off. "We both had, uh, family issues."

That sounded a bit suspicious. I was about to pry further, but Abdul jumped up and shouted, "Hey Shawn, over here!"

I watched as Shawn carried his tray toward our table. I couldn't help but reflect how much things had changed in such a short period of time. Just one week ago, my friends hated Shawn's guts. Now they were all buddy buddy with him. Heck, now *I* was buddy buddy with him.

Shawn had just walked past the Dunce's table when Jasper grabbed his arm and said, "Hey, where you going, man? We have plenty of room, sit with us!"

Rufus and Cletus opened their mouths in

shock, causing food to fall out. It was sort of gross to watch.

"Really?" Shawn asked suspiciously. "Why?"

"What do you mean why?" Jasper scoffed. "We've been best friends since kindergarten. Hopefully you didn't take our hazing seriously. We were just messing with you because your dad was trying to marry O'Connell's mom. But we're done with that now, it got old pretty quick. C'mon, sit!"

Shawn glanced at me. "I don't know, Jasper."

Jasper pointed toward us and said, "You really don't wanna keep sitting with those losers, do ya?"

Shawn seemed conflicted.

"C'mon, Shawn. Sit with us," Rufus pleaded.

"Yeah, we miss you," Cletus whined.

I couldn't blame Rufus and Cletus for wanting Shawn back as their leader. He was probably a lot nicer to them than Jasper was.

Shawn glanced at me one last time before doing the unthinkable: he sat with the Dunces. I was stunned.

"The nerve of that guy," Penelope growled, stabbing her meatloaf with her fork. "I knew we couldn't trust him."

Blake clutched his chest. "I thought Shawn and I were bffs. I'm heartbroken!"

"I'm never talking to that slimeball again, even if he does become your brother," Abdul muttered.

"Don't worry, that won't happen," I replied. "I'm now more determined than ever to stop this wedding."

"If you need our help, we're here for you," Penelope said.

I began to sweat. I seriously wanted to ask Penelope out. I'd been thinking about it ever since April dumped me. I figured this was as good a time as any.

Stuttering like a nervous idiot, I said, "Penelope, would you like to go to my mom's wedding with me? As my date? I mean, I'm still hoping she calls it off, but in case she doesn't, would you go with me?"

Everyone at our table gasped. Penelope dropped her fork on the ground. She leaned across the table and grabbed my hand. I immediately knew something was wrong because Penelope was never the touchy feeling type.

"Harold, I would, but..." Penelope turned her head to the side. "I'm seeing someone else."

I yanked my hand back. My palm was so sweaty I had to wipe it on my jeans.

"Oh, that's cool," I said, trying to sound like it didn't bother me. "So who are you seeing?"

"She's going out with me, Fat-Man," Ben said with a mouthful of meatloaf.

I tried not to lose my temper, but I couldn't help it.

"Are you serious?!" I exploded. "Why would you date Ben? You hate Ben!"

"Not cool, Fat-Man," Ben grumbled.

I lunged across the table and grabbed Ben by his shirt. "I'm gonna kick your butt, you scrawny little..."

Abdul and Blake pulled me back. Everyone within hearing distance looked at us, including Shawn and the Dunces. Jasper gulped. He probably thought I was some violent, crazy person now.

Coach Farmer hurried over and asked, "You guys okay? I heard a bunch of commotion over here."

"Yeah, we're fine, Coach," Penelope said, forcing a smile.

Coach glanced around. "Say, where's Shawn?"

"With the Dunces," Abdul grumbled.

Coach looked over at the Dunces' table and gasped. "Well I'll be," he mumbled.

Someone threw a paper airplane at Coach's head, breaking his train of thought. Coach ran to the other side of the cafeteria to yell at the kid who threw it.

Abdul was still clutching my shirt. "You okay, Harold? Can I let you go?"

I raised my hands. "Yeah, I'm cool."

As soon as Abdul let go of me, I lunged across the table. Ben yelped and fell out of his chair.

Penelope slammed her fist on my hand. I cried out in pain and sat back down.

"Quit attacking my boyfriend!" Penelope shouted.

"But I don't understand!" I cried. "Ben always got on your nerves. How could you go out with him? And how could you not tell me?"

"He asked me out a couple days after you started dating April," Penelope explained quietly. "We were going to tell you, but then April dumped you. We didn't want to rub our relationship in your face while you were down in the dumps."

"You knew about this the entire time?" I asked Abdul.

Abdul lowered his head and quietly replied, "Maybe."

I stood up. "Okay. So that's how it's going

to be, huh? I thought you all were my friends. I guess I was wrong. You guys are no better than Shawn."

"Harold," Penelope started to say.

I never found out what she was going to say because a carton of milk exploded against the back of my head. I twirled around to find the Dunces cackling like psychotic lunatics. Shawn wasn't laughing, but he sure didn't stick up for me. Coach was at the front of the cafeteria. I knew he'd seen what happened, but when I stared at him, he turned away. Now everyone was against me.

I stormed out of the cafeteria as my world shattered around me.

Chapter Seventeen

Football practice was pretty rough, especially since I was mad at everyone. Penelope and the gang tried to chat with me as we did stretches, but I walked to the other side of the field. Unfortunately, I wasn't paying enough attention because I soon found myself doing toe-stretches next to Shawn and the Dunces. I quickly ran to the front of the field. But that wasn't much better because Coach Farmer was up there, looking over his playbook. Coach glanced up and tried to talk to me, too, but I was mad at him for not shouting at the Dunces when they threw milk at me. I wound up stretching next to Coach Heffer while he gorged on cheese conies. You knew my life had taken a turn for the worst when I was hanging out with the worst coach in America.

Mom didn't show up for practice because she was so busy planning for the wedding. Granny picked up me and my friends (or maybe I should say 'acquaintances', since we weren't really friends at the moment) after practice and took us home. Coach Farmer made Shawn go home with me, which I was actually fine with. I could finally confront him about his reunion with the Dunces.

On the way home, no one said a word. It was one of the most uncomfortable rides of my life. Granny sensed something was wrong, probably because we were usually all loud and obnoxious.

"You can cut the tension in here with a

knife. What's wrong with you kids? You all sick or something?"

"No Granny, we're just tired," I said. "Coach had us practicing hard."

Granny dropped off my friends... er, I mean, 'acquaintances'... and drove me and Shawn home. After she pulled into the driveway, she took the keys out of the ignition and looked at me suspiciously.

"Seriously, what's going on?"

"Nothing," I grumbled.

Granny rolled her eyes and wobbled out of the car. "Whatevs. Go do your little 'study date' shtick. I'll be up shortly so we can figure out how we're gonna stop this dang wedding. It's almost become an obsession for me."

Shawn and I followed Granny into the house. As usual, we walked straight into total chaos. The whole family was there, as well as a bunch of people I never met. I quickly figured out the strangers were wedding planners. (Coach's brother must have already hired them.) The planners were going over all sorts of things with Mom, including floral arrangements, the wedding cake, and Mom's wedding gown. The aunts were there, too. I could tell they were a bit frazzled by everything going on because they kept gulping down coffee like there was no tomorrow.

Adding to the craziness, Jon and Anthony ran around the house with their pants off, blasting each other with water pistols. Betty chased after them, barking and wagging her tail. Granny grabbed her super soaker out of the sink and joined in.

Great Granny was out in the backyard, whacking weeds with her weed whacker. Chucky and his pals were in the basement, practicing a new rock song. Mom said they could be the musical entertainment at the wedding. I think she was just trying to save money.

I led Shawn upstairs without saying a word. When we got to my room, I plopped down on my bed and twiddled my thumbs. Shawn sat on a chair and did the same thing. We were quiet for a *long* time.

Shawn was the first to speak. "I don't know why you're upset. Isn't this what we wanted? For things to go back to normal?"

"I don't know what you're talking about," I said. "I'm not mad."

"Oh please. You were totally mad when I sat with the Dunces."

"Well, why wouldn't I be?" I replied bluntly. "After everything they've said and done to me... after everything they said and did to you... and you sat with them just because they started talking to you again?"

"You're just jealous because my friends aren't losers like yours!"

I gritted my teeth. "You are such an idiot. You do realize Jasper is just trying to get back at me for tackling him, right?"

Shawn scoffed. "That makes no sense. What, did you think we were friends or something? We've only been hanging out so we can stop this stupid wedding. We were never friends. We never will be friends."

I was surprised by how much Shawn's words hurt me. I didn't let him know that, though. "At least you and I agree on one thing. I'll never be friends with a back-stabbing, two-faced jerk."

"I'm two-faced?!" Shawn exploded. "You dressed up like a mop-haired vampire freak just so you could impress April Summers! You're the fakest person I know. Penelope was falling head-over-heels for you, but you ignored her so you could snag a date with someone you thought was prettier. And then when April dumped you, you went crawling back to Penelope. Oh yes, I watched you ask her out at lunch. Did you seriously think she'd go out with you? No girl wants to feel like they're your second or third choice."

Part of me was so angry at Shawn that I wanted to punch his lights out. But another part realized at least some of what he said was true. No wonder Penelope decided to go out with Ben. I had turned into a big phony who blew her off for someone I thought was better. I became everything I couldn't stand.

I had too much pride to admit Shawn was kinda right, so instead I said, "Why would you want to hang with the Dunces again? You heard all the horrible things Jasper said about my friends. You heard what he said about Chucky."

Shawn shrugged. "I don't like it when he talks like that, either. But it was just talk. It's not like he was really going to call immigration and have Penelope's family deported." Under his breath, he added, "At least, I don't think he would."

"If that's him joking around, I'd hate to see him when he's serious," I said.

I tried to control my anger, but I couldn't help myself. I shoved Shawn so hard that he fell backwards and bumped into my TV.

"You jerk!" Shawn returned the shove, knocking me on my bed. I jumped up and tackled Shawn to the floor. We rolled around like a couple of wrestlers, slapping each other, pulling hair, and shouting insults.

I don't know how long we fought, but we were eventually separated when Granny barged in and yanked us apart.

"Knock it off!" Granny hollered.

I let go of Shawn and plopped back down on my bed. Shawn sat in his chair.

"What's the matter with you two?" Granny chastised. "We don't have time for this nonsense. We have a wedding to stop, remember? You can have your little pillow fight next week, after the wedding is nothing but a distant memory."

"You're right, Granny," I grumbled, clutching my throbbing head. Shawn hit me pretty hard.

"What do you think we should do, Granny?" Shawn asked, nursing his wrist.

Granny grinned. "Remember when I told you how I stopped my mother's wedding?"

"Oh no," I groaned.

"Oh yes," Granny chortled.

Granny grabbed both of us by our collars and pulled us so close I could smell the limburger cheese on her breath. (Grannies always seemed to eat nasty stuff.) Granny then rattled off her crazy plan to stop my mom's wedding once and for all.

Chapter Eighteen

School the rest of the week was awkward and stressful. I was so mad at Penelope, Ben, and Shawn that I barely spoke to any of them unless it was absolutely necessary (like when Shawn was blocking my path in the hallway and I said, "Move it, jerk.").

Shawn quickly went back to his old ways. I learned that the hard way in Ms. Hornswaggle's class. I was dozing off like I normally did, when a sopping wet spitball exploded against my cheek. I yelped and fell out of my seat. Everyone pointed and laughed, even Penelope and the gang. April shouted, "Loser!"

Ms. Meow Meow scurried over and hissed.

Ms. Hornswaggle peered at me over the top of her bifocals. "Another outburst in class, Mr. O'Connell? Seriously, what is the matter with you? Do you have some sort of debilitating mental disorder I don't know about?"

"But... I... Shawn..."

Ms. Hornswaggle whipped out a pink slip and shrieked, "Detention!"

I groaned and banged my head on my desk as Ms. Meow Meow brought me my slip. Ms. Hornswaggle spun around and scribbled some nonsense about how kids who read ended up more successful than people who didn't. I begged to differ. Video games gave you street smarts, which everyone needs to survive in a dangerous world.

Lunch was weird because Penelope and Ben didn't sit with me. Blake and Abdul did, though, and I was extremely grateful. I hated sitting by myself. We didn't talk about what happened the day before. We just chatted about comic books and wrestling.

Shawn sat with the Dunces again. The Dunces started throwing stuff at us. We fired back. Coach Farmer ran over and hollered. The Dunces left us alone after that.

Gym was god-awful, as always. Coach Bebop and Coach Heffer didn't pay much attention to us. They were too busy going over the playbook for our game later that afternoon. They made us play dodge ball, which turned out to be a horrible experience for me. Shawn, April, Ben, Penelope, and all three Dunces bombarded me with balls at the exact same time. I collapsed in an unmoving heap.

Our last game of the season was away at Nixon Academy, so Coach Farmer had us gather in the locker room before we boarded the bus. Coach went on to give a sappy speech about how proud he was of us, and how he enjoyed watching us turn into fine young men (and in Penelope's case, a fine young lady who could kick serious butt). I think Coach was trying to motivate us into playing as hard as we could, so we would scratch out a win and he wouldn't be completely embarrassed.

It didn't work. We ended up losing 56-3. I was *soooo* glad our season was over.

I was so exhausted from my hectic week that I slept until 2:00pm Saturday afternoon, just in time for Coach Farmer's bachelor party.

Now I only knew about bachelor parties

from what I saw on movies and TV shows. They looked like a heck of a lot of fun, but I knew my mom would never let me go to one. So I was understandably suspicious when Mom said I could go to Coach Farmer's party. She also said Jon and Anthony could go, as well as my friends. That only increased my suspicion.

Mom, Great Granny, and the aunts were going to spend the day shopping and having a bachelorette lunch. (Mom hated parties.) Granny couldn't go because she had 'other plans'. While they were out, Chucky drove me, Jon, and Anthony to Coach Heffer's house (where the party was being held). Coach Heffer lived down the street from us in a trailer park. It didn't seem like the sort of place you'd have a bachelor party, but what did I know?

Outside the trailer park, a bunch of shirtless guys were grilling out. Their wives sat on lawn chairs with curlers in their hair. A bunch of shirtless kids ran around, throwing rocks at each other. Dogs, cats, and pet raccoons chased after them. (At least, I think the raccoons were pets because they were wearing collars.)

"Yep, these are definitely Coach Heffer's people," I said.

Chucky parked the car next to Heffer's trailer. The outside was decorated with blinking Christmas lights… in September.

Abdul and Blake were already there. They were standing outside when we walked up. Jon and Anthony ran off to throw rocks with the kids.

Abdul burst out laughing. "Dude, this is like the worst bachelor party ever."

"Oh really?" I said. "You've been to a lot of bachelor parties?"

"No, but I know how they're supposed to be,

and they definitely ain't like this."

I glanced around and frowned. "So I take it Penelope and Ben aren't coming?"

Blake giggled. "No silly, they hate your guts."

Abdul shoved Blake into the trailer before he said anything else. Chucky and I followed them.

I wasn't quite sure what to expect when I first entered Coach Heffer's trailer, but it definitely wasn't this. It looked more like a 5-year old's birthday celebration than a bachelor party. I expected to see a bunch of adult games. Instead there was pin-the-tail-on-the-donkey, twister, and hillbilly golf.

Coach Farmer was sitting on the couch, talking to a bald, middle-aged dude wearing a sleeveless shirt. He had a brown goatee and a bulging hairy belly.

Coach Bebop was there as well. She was leaning against the wall with her arms crossed. She looked miserable. It was probably because some sleazy dude wearing an unbuttoned Hawaiian shirt was hitting on her.

Shawn sat at a table, looking deathly bored. He glanced at me for a brief moment before looking away.

Coach Heffer waddled over and said, "Hey kids! Welcome to my humble abode."

"Hi, Coach. Your place is… nice," I lied.

"Thanks, kiddo. It may not be much, but it's all mine. Here, let me introduce you to everyone." Coach Heffer pointed to the fat bald dude sitting on the couch next to Coach Farmer. "That's our best pal from elementary school, Carl."

"How y'all doing?" Carl grunted as he scratched himself. I could have sworn I saw a flea hopping around on his hairy belly.

Coach Heffer pointed to the sleazy dude. "And that's our old pal, Roger."

Roger nodded his head like he was cool or something. "S'up?"

"S'up?" I said, mocking him.

I glanced around and noticed no one else was there. "Gee, you guys don't have a lot of friends, do you?"

"It's not the number of friends you have, it's the quality," Coach Farmer replied philosophically.

"Yeah," Carl said. He then burped and scratched himself again.

Coach Bebop sighed heavily. "Why did you invite me here, Sam? Women usually aren't invited to bachelor parties."

"But you're my best man," Coach Farmer said.

Coach Heffer held up Candyland. "Who wants to play a game?"

Everyone in the trailer groaned.

"This bachelor party is so stupid," Carl griped. "Where's the adult games? Where's the dancers? And for crying out loud, why are there kids here? I hate kids!"

"I'm sure kids aren't too fond of you either, Carl," Shawn said.

"Carl's got a point though," Roger said. "This party is lame. What gives?"

"Penny doesn't approve of raunchy bachelor parties," Coach Farmer explained. "She said the only way I could have one was if I made it PG and invited the kids."

Carl made the sound of a cracking whip. "We now know who wears the pants in this relationship."

"At least I'm in a relationship," Coach Farmer said defensively.

"He got you there, Carl!" sleazy Roger cackled. He nudged Coach Bebop in the side. "Didn't he, Bertha? Didn't he?"

"Don't touch me," Coach Bebop snapped.

"I already explained this to you guys," Carl grumbled. "Girls are intimidated by me because of my dashing good looks and irresistible charm."

"Are you sure it's not your irresistible body odor?" I cracked, pinching my nose. Coach Bebop gave me a hi-five for that one.

Carl brushed off the potato chip crumbs stuck in his belly hair. "Sorry Sam, but I didn't come here to babysit. C'mon Roger, let's go find another party to crash."

Carl and Roger were just about to leave when I hollered, "Wait, don't go! The entertainment hasn't arrived yet."

"What entertainment?" Coach Farmer asked. "I didn't set anything up."

"Of course not. Shawn and I did."

Coach Farmer was about to say something, but the doorbell cut him off. I opened the door and gasped. Granny burst into the trailer wearing a blue police uniform.

Granny twirled a pair of handcuffs around her index finger and said, "You guys have the right to get crazy!"

I stared at Granny in horror. Shawn nudged her in the side and said, "I thought you were hiring a dancer."

"I figured this would be cheaper," Granny replied.

"Oh no," Coach Farmer cried, struggling to get up off the couch.

"Oh yes," Granny said. She whipped out her night-stick and whacked Coach upside the back of his head.

"Granny, don't hit him!" I shouted.

"Sorry, I've been watching too many episodes of *Cops* lately," Granny said.

Carl and Roger greedily rubbed their hands.

"Haha, now we're talking," Carl gushed. "*This* is a bachelor party."

Granny took off her hat and put it on Coach Farmer's head.

"Quick, take a picture," I said to Shawn.

Shawn whipped out his cellphone.

"Give him a kiss, Granny," I said.

"No, don't give me a kiss," Coach Farmer hollered. He shoved Granny to the side and ran out the front door.

"Don't let him get away, Granny," I said. "We need to get a picture!"

"I'm on it," Granny said, waddling after him.

Thankfully, Coach Farmer tripped over one of Coach Heffer's lawn chairs. That allowed Granny to catch up to him.

"Why you running away?" Granny asked, waving her night-stick in the air. "This is what Penny's going to look like in 30 years. You better get used to it now."

Coach screamed and scrambled to his feet. Shawn and I ran after him.

"Dad, wait!" Shawn shouted.

Coach ran out into the middle of the street without looking. A minivan plowed into him. Coach flew up over the hood and slammed into the van's windshield. The minivan skidded to a halt. Coach flew off the windshield and collapsed onto the ground in a crumpled heap.

"Dad!" Shawn screamed.

We ran over to Coach and gasped. His right leg was bent backwards. I didn't need to be a pre-med student like Chad Michaels to know it was broken.

Mom jumped out of the minivan and ran over, screaming hysterically.

I looked up at Mom and stuttered, "M...Mom? W... what are you doing here?"

Mom didn't hear me. She knelt down and cradled Coach's head in her arms. The aunts hurried over as well, followed by Great Granny.

"Oh my goodness," Aunt Patty cried, covering her eyes.

Great Granny glanced at Coach Farmer's leg and flapped her wrist. "Ah, he'll be fine. Just pour rubbing alcohol over the wound and send him off to bed."

"I don't think rubbing alcohol heals broken bones," I said.

"That's what's wrong with this generation," Great Granny griped. "Everybody is over-medicated."

I shook my head and said, "I thought you guys were going shopping and having a bachelorette lunch."

"We were," Aunty Kathy said. "But Penny forgot her wallet, so we had to come back."

"Will somebody please call a freaking ambulance," Coach Farmer whimpered.

"I'm on it," Coach Bebop said, whipping out her phone.

"How on Earth did this happen?" Mom sobbed, wiping her tear-filled eyes. "Why did Sam run out in the middle of the street?"

"I have no clue," Granny said, still twirling her night-stick.

Mom, Great Granny, and the aunts stared at Granny in confusion. They were probably wondering why she was dressed like a cop.

"Okay guys, seriously, what is going on here?" Mom asked sternly.

Great Granny grabbed Granny by her ear. "I think I know. This reminds me of when Darlene ruined my wedding 20 years ago."

Mom narrowed her eyes. "Why are you trying to ruin my wedding, Mother?"

"I'll never tell," Granny said.

Great Granny twisted Granny's ear. Granny cried, "Okay, okay, Harold and Shawn made me do it! It was their idea!"

"Granny!" I hollered.

Mom shot me the look of death. "Harold O'Connell! This is enough! You listen to me and you listen to me *good*, buster. I am marrying Sam, and there's *nothing* you can do about it. I don't care if we have to push Sam down the aisle in a wheelchair, I am getting married tomorrow."

"But Mom…"

"No buts, Harold. You are grounded until you're 30!"

"Don't you think that's a bit excessive, babe?" Coach Farmer groaned.

"Sam, he broke your leg."

"Actually Mom, you were the one who…"

Mom shot me another evil look. I gulped and shut up.

The ambulance arrived a few seconds later. Mom and Shawn went with Coach to the hospital while Aunt Kathy drove the rest of us home in the minivan. The entire time Great Granny hollered about how Granny and I were so busted. She said Granny was grounded until she was 90. Granny grumbled something about how her mother was totally lame.

As soon as I got home, I went straight to bed. I needed to make sure I got plenty of sleep for what was sure to be the worst day of my life.

Chapter Nineteen


The next day was Mom's wedding, otherwise known as Doomsday. Everyone was still angry with me for almost killing Coach Farmer, even Granny. She blamed me for Great Granny grounding her.

The worst part of it was that Mom didn't talk to me at all. You'd think she'd at least say two words to her oldest child on the day of her wedding, but nope; by the time I woke up, she was long gone. According to Great Granny (the only grownup still speaking to me), Mom and the aunts headed to the church at the crack of dawn to get everything ready. Chucky and his friends left, too, I guess to set up their instruments.

Mom wanted us to look nice, so I put on my only suit and tie. We didn't have too many weddings or fancy gatherings in my family, so my suit was pretty old. I had grown quite a bit since the last time I wore it, vertically and horizontally, so it barely fit. My belly bulged out and the buttons looked like they were about to pop loose. Great Granny said I could borrow her girdle, but I politely declined and sucked in my tummy instead.

It took my grannies forever to get Jon and Anthony ready (they kept smacking each other with their ties). Once they did, we made sure Betty had plenty of food and water and headed out to the minivan.

We hadn't been in the car five seconds when

Jon and Anthony took off their ties and started hitting each other again. I did my best to ignore them and stared out the window.

After everything that happened over the past few weeks, I should have been down and out. Everything I did ended in disaster. But I was actually cautiously optimistic that, despite all the setbacks, Mom's wedding would still be stopped. I was cutting it a lot closer than I would have liked, but thanks to Shawn we had one last ace up our sleeves.

Shawn called it our 'nuclear option'. I didn't even know about it until late last night, several hours after I first fell asleep. My phone buzzed around 2:00am. Even though it was on vibrate, it still made a ton of noise as it rattled around on top of my nightstand. I groggily answered it. Needless to say, I was shocked when Shawn's voice whispered, "We need to talk."

I put aside all the pent-up animosity I felt toward Shawn and listened as he rambled on about our last, best chance to stop the wedding. Shawn explained that he came up with it shortly after our disastrous camping trip. He never told me about it because that was the day we started fighting.

Shawn's 'nuclear option' was just like our first plan: use the internet to find love for our folks. In Shawn's words, it was time to get back to basics.

What he did was call up my granny and casually ask who my mom's high school sweetheart was. Granny was in the middle of her soap operas, so she quickly told him so he'd leave her alone. Shawn already knew who his dad used to date because he mentioned her before. He then looked up our parents' high school sweethearts on the internet. Fortunately they both still lived in the area.

Shawn went on to create Facebook accounts for our folks. (Neither of them had one because they liked to pretend it was still 1999. Even my freaking granny was on Facebook.) After the accounts were activated, Shawn sent a message to Mom's high school crush. He also sent one to Coach Farmer's. Both messages basically said our parents were about to be married, but they still had feelings for their old high school flames. If the 'flames' felt the same way, they should come interrupt the wedding ceremony right after the exchanging of the vows.

Now on paper Shawn's plan looked insane. But that was why it was so brilliant. Hopefully our parents would be so confused and conflicted that they postponed the wedding. That would at least buy us more time.

The church was down the street, so we got there in no time. The parking lot was super crowded when we first pulled in. I noticed a bunch of senior citizens waddling in with their canes. Granny must have invited all her pals from the senior center.

We all got out of the car and made our way inside. The church was small, so we were all squished together like sardines. I noticed Penelope and Ben off in the corner, talking. It meant a lot to me that they showed up. Their parents probably dragged them along since they were invited, too, but I was still glad to see them. Penelope looked especially pretty in her lavender dress. I'd have to tell her. Maybe that would break the wall that built up between us.

I was surprised to see Uncle Bob and Oinky out in the reception area. Uncle Bob was setting up buffet tables for the party afterwards. Coach Farmer's brother must have hired him to do the catering. If he knew my family was going to be involved, he probably wouldn't have taken the job. Poor Oinky shivered in fear when he saw us.

Granny waved and hollered, "Hey Bob! Hey Oinky!"

Oinky squealed and ran off down the hall. Uncle Bob, however, blushed and waved back. I didn't expect that.

Jon and Anthony were part of the wedding, so they went into the back. Great Granny led me and Granny into the main part of the church where all the pews were. Most of the pews were packed. We found a few empty spots near the middle.

I whipped out my phone and glanced at the time. The wedding was set to start in ten minutes. Sweat poured from my armpits. It wasn't just because the church was hot, either. I was nervous about Shawn's crazy plan. The more I thought about it, the more paranoid I got. So I tried to stop thinking about it. (That didn't work.)

Over the next ten minutes, the pews became even more packed. Pretty soon I was squished between my grannies. I watched as Penelope and Ben sat across the aisle from us. The sight of them holding hands made me want to hurl chunks, so I looked away. A few rows up, Abdul sat with his mom and dad. Blake and his family sat next to them.

Coach Farmer was up in the very front, sitting in a wheelchair. He had on a tuxedo and bowtie, and his right leg was in a cast. He kept smiling and staring at his hand. He must have been on a lot of painkillers.

Chucky and his band mates were up in the pulpit area, playing music. It wasn't classical wedding music, either, but some of their hard rock stuff. Great Granny kept mumbling about how rock wasn't appropriate in a house of God.

About a minute later, all the bridesmaids and groomsmen started walking down the aisle. Coach Bebop walked with Coach Heffer. Coach Heffer was already crying, but Coach Bebop looked deathly bored. Carl came out next with Aunt Patty. I snickered at the sight of Carl's bulging, hairy belly popping out of his tuxedo.

Sleazy Roger and Aunt Kathy walked out after them. Roger's hair was even greasier than usual, and he had on an orange suit and blue tie. He made my eyes hurt.

Jon ran down the aisle next, sprinkling flowers all over the place. Mom couldn't find a real flower girl, so she decided to use him.

Little Anthony scampered out after that, carrying two gleaming wedding rings on a pillow. Everyone went, "Awwwww," when he walked by.

Granny clutched my left arm. "Isn't he just precious?"

Great Granny grabbed my right arm. "Isn't he adorable?"

I squirmed out of both my grannies' grasp. "No, he's an annoying brat."

My grannies scoffed and smacked me with their purses.

Chucky and the gang suddenly burst into a hard-rock version of *Here Comes The Bride.* Everyone jumped to their feet and snapped pictures as Mom appeared in the doorway.

My jaw fell open in shock. I would never say this to my friends or the kids at school, but my mom looked beautiful. Her dress was as white as snow. The bottom trailed behind her like a flowing cape. A lace veil covered her face. She also clutched a bouquet of flowers. The flowers looked a lot better than the ones I gave April.

Mom slowly made her way down the aisle. Cameras continued to flash, blinding me. Halfway to the pulpit, Anthony ran over and hugged her legs.

"You look pretty, Mommy," he said.

Once again everyone went, "Awwwww." My grannies bawled like babies.

Mom stood across from Coach Farmer and smiled. Coach blushed.

The pastor stepped forward and waved at Chucky. Chucky and his pals stopped playing and took a bow.

Chucky grabbed a microphone and said, "We'll be playing next week at the County Fair's Battle of the Bands competition. Come cheer us on so we can win new guitars."

"Er, thank you, Charles," the pastor said.

The pastor looked like an older version of Shawn, except his hair was gray. His name was Maxwell Robinson and he was Shawn's uncle. (Shawn's mom was Maxwell's sister.) We all just called him Pastor Max. Pastor Max had always been nice to me and my family, so I liked him a lot.

Pastor Max folded his hands and waited for all the mumbling and camera flashes to die down. Once it was deathly quiet, he said, in a deep, booming voice, "We are gathered here today to celebrate the glorious love between…"

I didn't hear much after that because I was beginning to get nervous about Shawn's 'nuclear option'. My heart was beating so hard and fast that it rang in my ears. I was vaguely aware of Mom and Coach Farmer exchanging their vows and Anthony handing them their rings.

I finally snapped back to reality when Mom and Coach said, "I do."

Pastor Max smiled and gestured toward all of us in the pews.

"Before I make this blessed union official in the eyes of God, is there anyone who believes this happy couple should not be wed? If so, speak now or forever hold your peace."

The next few seconds seemed to unfold like hours. No one said a word. I kept turning around and glancing at the door. This was Shawn's cue. Where the heck was he?

Pastor Max said, "Since no one objects, I know pronounce you husband and..."

"STOP!"

Everyone in the church spun around and watched as Shawn burst through the front door. He was followed by a balding, chubby dude who I assumed was Mom's old high school boyfriend, Paul Diamond. Behind him was a short, red-haired woman. That must have been Coach Farmer's old flame, Sarah Lung.

"Shawn? Wha... what are you doing?" sputtered Pastor Max.

"Sorry, Uncle," Shawn said, marching up the aisle. "But I have to stop my dad and Ms. O'Connell from making a huge mistake."

Everyone in the church started murmuring.

Granny clapped her hands. "Oh, how exciting! Stuff like this always happens during weddings on my soap operas."

When Shawn reached my row, he pointed at me and said, "I'm not doing this alone, O'Connell. Get your butt over here."

I gulped and climbed over Granny's lap.

Coach Farmer looked at us in confusion. I think the painkillers he was taking were still messing with his brain. Mom, however, looked downright furious.

"So it's not enough you chased my fiancé into oncoming traffic?" Mom snarled. "Now you have to interrupt our wedding? Have you no shame, Harold O'Connell?"

I felt my face turn red. I hated it when Mom yelled at me in public.

"Mom, I'm just trying to stop you from doing something you're going to regret. Coach is not your type. He's dumb and smelly and dumb and stupid and... well, dumb!"

"Hey," Coach griped. "I don't smell."

"And Dad, you can do so much better than Ms. O'Connell," Shawn said. "She's not all that."

"Why I never!" Mom exclaimed.

I could tell Mom was about to blow a gasket, so I pulled Paul in front of me and said, "Look, Shawn and I found your old high school sweetheart, Paul Ruby."

"My last name is Diamond," Paul said.

"Whatever dude, it's not important," I grumbled.

Mom's face went from volcano red to snow-white in about two seconds.

"Paul? Oh my gosh, is that really you?"

"Yes, Penny," Paul said, giving her a hug. He even picked her off the ground and twirled her around. Mom giggled. Coach Farmer growled.

"Wow, you look beautiful," Paul gushed.

Sarah Lung rushed up to Coach and gave him a peck on the cheek. "And you look just as handsome as I remember, Sam."

Coach Farmer blushed and giggled, this time causing Mom to growl. "Aw shucks, you're still perty, too, Sarah."

I clapped and said, "Wow, it's probably

been years since you guys last talked. Why don't we cancel the wedding and you old lovebirds catch up on old times?"

Mom held up her hand. "Wait a minute. Now Paul, don't take this the wrong way; I'm thrilled to see you and I'd love to catch up sometime, but... why are you here?"

"I was just about to ask the same thing," Coach Farmer said to Sarah.

Paul scratched his thinning head. "What do you mean? You're the ones who asked us to come."

"Do what?" Mom exclaimed.

"Yeah, you guys messaged us on Facebook and said if we wanted another shot at our high school romance, we should interrupt your wedding," Sarah explained breathlessly.

Mom glared at me. I could have sworn I saw her green irises glow fiery red.

"Harold, you and I are going to have a long, *loooong* talk later tonight."

I gulped. Mom's 'long talks' were usually her yelling at me for five hours straight. I'd have to find some ear plugs.

Mom turned to Paul Diamond and forced a smile. "I'm sorry, Paul, but there's been a terrible misunderstanding. I never sent you a message. I'm not even on Facebook. My evil genius son over there must have e-mailed you."

"Actually, Shawn's the one who did it," I said.

Shawn nudged me in the side. "Shut up, dude."

Mom gave me another dose of the evil eye before turning back to Paul. "I would love to catch up with you sometime, Paul, and it's great to see you again, it really is. But I'm about to marry my fiancé. You and Sarah are more than welcome to stay. We're going to have a huge reception afterwards with lots of food."

"Oh, I love food," Sarah giggled.

"Me too," Paul said.

I threw my hands in the air and said, "Yeah yeah, we all love food. But Paul, isn't there something you want to say to my mom? Before she gets married and you have to 'forever hold your peace'?

Paul thought for a second, then said, "Nope, nothing comes to mind."

My left eye twitched. "Paul, isn't the entire reason you're here because you still have feelings for my mom? Don't you want to tell her how much you love her?"

"You… you love me?" Mom sputtered.

"Of course I love you," Paul said. "Or, I *did* love you. But it really has been a long time, hasn't it? We may not even be the same people anymore. The more I think about it, the more this whole thing seems pretty crazy. I don't know what I was thinking. I guess I was just so excited to hear from you that I momentarily lost my mind."

"Me too," Sarah said, blushing.

"But as it turns out, you guys really didn't message us, did you?" Paul said.

"No, I'm sorry. We did not," Mom said sadly.

Paul grabbed Mom's hands and smiled. "Hey, don't be sad. Sarah and I were just out in the hall talking and… well, we really seemed to hit it off. We even talked about going out to dinner next week."

Sarah giggled. "Oh Paul, you know just what to say to make me blush."

"That's great!" Coach Farmer said, bouncing around excitedly in his wheelchair. "We should all go on a double date after I get this dang cast off."

"Oh, what happened to your leg?" Sarah asked, as if she noticed for the first time that Coach was in a wheelchair.

Coach pointed at me. "His grandmother tried to kill me!"

Granny jumped up and said, "Your fiancé is the one who ran you over!"

Mom, Coach, Granny, Paul, and Sarah all started talking at once.

I slapped my forehead. I couldn't believe things spiraled out of control so quickly. How come none of my master plans ever went the way they were supposed to? I mean seriously, what the heck? Now I knew how Doctor Platypus felt every time Assassin Grandma thwarted his plans for world domination.

"Everyone please be quiet!" I exploded.

The church became eerily quiet.

I cleared my throat and said, "Mom, please, can we hold off on the wedding for just one more day? So we can talk?"

Mom shook her head so fiercely, her veil whipped back and forth. "No, Harold, absolutely not. I love Sam with all my heart and I want to spend the rest of my life with him. Why can't you accept that? Why can't you…"

Mom's voice cracked as her eyes welled up with tears.

"Why can't you accept my happiness?"

"What about my happiness, Mom? What about the rest of the family? What if we don't want two more people moving in with us? Our house is crazy enough as it is."

Tears continued streaming down her cheeks, but Mom's tone was now angry.

"You have got to be the most selfish person I know, Harold. I thought my mother was selfish, but she doesn't hold a candle to you."

"Hey," Granny started to say.

"Shush it, Mother!" Mom snapped. "I'll get to you in a minute."

"But Mom...," I stammered.

"No Harold, let me finish. You are so incredibly selfish. You think this is all about you. It isn't. I should get to decide who I want to spend the rest of my life with, not you. I would never dream of telling you who to marry. Your selfishness is the reason you lost all your friends. It's why you lost your girlfriend. And it's about to tear our family apart."

Everyone in the church stared at Mom in shock. She sure let me have it. And I was about to give it right back.

"I think I get it now." I was speaking quietly, but since no one else was talking, my voice echoed throughout the church. "I know why you're remarrying. You don't love Dad anymore. Well I'm sorry, Mom, but I'm not going to stop loving Dad just because he's *dead*."

Everyone gasped. Pastor Max made the sign of the cross.

Mom's eyes turned into raging waterfalls. "Oh Harold..."

Mom picked up the bottom of her dress and rushed down the aisle. People in the pews stood up and watched. The church became filled with the sounds of dozens of people murmuring at the same time.

"Mom?" I said, walking after her.

Mom burst through the front doors and started running.

"Mom!" I shouted.

Someone gripped my arm. I spun around and came face to face with Coach Farmer.

"That was totally uncalled for, Harold. You know your Mom loves your father."

My chest began to ache. I couldn't believe I said such a mean thing to my mother. I couldn't help myself; it just sort of came out, like vomit.

I pulled out of Coach's grasp. "I... I know. I'm sorry. I... I gotta go talk to her."

I spun around and nearly collided with Shawn.

"Let me help," he said. "This is sorta my fault."

"Okay," I said numbly. I still couldn't believe I told Mom she didn't love Dad. That was probably the worst thing I ever said.

Granny wobbled over to me and said, "What did you do?"

"What do you meant what did I do?" I snapped. "You were in on this, too. You're 62. I'm just a kid. You're supposed to stop me from doing stupid things, not help me!"

Granny and I started bickering. We stopped when Great Granny grabbed us both by our ears.

"Ouch!" Granny and I yelped.

"You two should be ashamed of yourselves," Great Granny chided us. "Ruining poor Penny's wedding... after everything she's done for this family. I know exactly how she feels. My daughter ruined my wedding 20 years ago."

Great Granny twisted Granny's ear.

"Ahhhh!" Granny hollered at the top of her

lungs. "Child abuse! Help!"

"Now get out there and fix what you broke." Great Granny shoved us stumbling down the aisle.

"Great Granny sure is violent," I huffed as Granny and I made our way out to the parking lot.

"She misses the 'good ole days' when corporal punishment was alive and well," Granny replied breathlessly.

When Granny and I reached the parking lot, we stopped to catch our breaths.

"I need to lose some weight," Granny said, bending over and clutching her knees.

"You and me both," I gasped, wiping sweat from my eyes.

I glanced around and frowned. "Where's Mom's car?"

Granny pointed to an empty parking space near the front. "It was there when we first arrived. She must already be gone."

I whipped out my cell phone and dialed Mom's number. My call went straight to her voicemail.

I kicked a rock. "Dang it, she could be anywhere."

By now a bunch of wedding guests had come outside. Shawn pushed Coach Farmer's wheelchair and they began looking for Mom, too.

"This is a disaster," I groaned. "Why couldn't I just keep my mouth shut?"

Granny patted me on the head. "It's genetic. Everyone on my side of the family has a malfunctioning social filter. Except my mother, of course. She's 'perfect'." Granny made quote marks with her fingers. I guess arguing with your mother was genetic, too.

Chucky rushed over and said, "I tried calling

Penny, but she's not answering. Anybody know where she could have gone?"

"I have no clue," I replied gloomily.

"Now let's not freak out yet," Granny said, pacing back and forth. "She couldn't have gone far. Let's think of some places she would go."

"Maybe she headed back to your guys' house," Shawn said, joining the huddle.

"Nah, that's too simple," I said. "She knows that would be the first place we'd look."

"Maybe she went to a friend's house?" Chucky suggested.

Granny shook her head. "All of her friends are here. Maybe she went to get a bucket of chicken?"

"Now why would she do that?" I asked.

Granny shrugged. "Whenever I'm stressed, I always get me a bucket of chicken."

I think I now knew why Granny had two chins.

We all shut up and racked our brains, struggling to figure out where Mom could have gone. That's when the light bulb in my head flickered on.

"Oh my gosh, I know where she went," I whispered.

"What?" Granny hollered.

"C'mon Granny, let's go!" I said, running toward her minivan. Granny, Shawn, and Chucky all followed me.

Granny hit the unlock button on her keys. All four of us opened the doors and climbed into the van.

"So where are we going?" Granny asked, shoving her key into the ignition.

"Dad's last resting place," I replied.

"Huh?" Shawn said.

Chucky and Granny knew what I meant.

"You know where you're going, Mom?" Chucky asked.

"I sure do, sonny," Granny said, backing out of the parking lot. She stepped on the gas and sped toward Spring Grove Cemetery.

Chapter Twenty

Spring Grove Cemetery was both the saddest and prettiest place in town. It was sad because so many lost loved ones were buried there. But it was beautiful because there were so many ancient gravesites and statues. There were also tons of trees, gardens, and fountains.

We pulled up to the front gate and slowly drove along the scenic trail that snaked through the giant cemetery. I knew I was supposed to keep an eye out for my mom, but I couldn't help pressing my face up against the window and looking at all the old tombs. There were a couple cool statues of Civil War soldiers on horses, towering over all the smaller graves.

There were also statues of scientists, politicians, business owners, and other locally famous people. Soaring over all those tombs were giant trees overflowing with red, yellow, and orange leaves. A cool fall breeze blew some of the leaves across the field of graves.

We eventually drove past a giant lake. Dozens of ducks and geese waddled around, foraging for food. Several fountains squirted water high into the air.

"Where's your dad's grave?" Shawn asked.

"We're almost there," I said. "It's near that giant fountain by the funeral home."

Shawn gasped. "Really? My... my mom's buried there."

"Oh," I said. All my anger toward Shawn seemed to melt away. "Well, you can visit your mom while I visit my dad."

Shawn sniffled. I didn't have to turn around to know he was blinking back tears. That's exactly what I was doing.

"I... I'd like to do that," he finally said.

"Here we are," Granny said suddenly.

The funeral home popped up over the horizon. As we got closer, I saw the giant fountain off to the side. A few people were sitting on the benches surrounding the fountain, watching the ducks. Across the street from the funeral home was another field of graves. There were a few people on the field paying their respects to the deceased. One of those people was sitting on the ground in a white wedding gown.

Mom.

Granny patted me on the head. "You were right, kiddo. You were right."

Granny parked along the curb, right behind Mom's car. Mom was near the middle of the field facing the other way, so she didn't see us.

We all got out of the van. Shawn thrust his hands in his pockets and said, "I'll, uh, be right back."

Shawn hurried to the other side of the field to visit his mother.

I started to make my way toward Mom. I stopped when I noticed Granny and Chucky weren't following me.

"You guys coming?" I called over my shoulder.

"Not just yet, hon," Granny said. "You talk to her first."

I nodded and continued walking toward my parents. I made sure not to step on the graves as I walked, as I heard that was disrespectful. A lot of the graves were decorated with flowers, birthday cards, photos, and candy. I always brought my dad a Snickers bar because he used to love them. I was sad I didn't have one to give him now.

I eventually reached Mom. She still didn't see me. She had her head in her hands and was quietly sobbing.

"Mom?" I said softly.

Mom looked up and turned around. Her eyes were red and her cheeks were wet.

"Harold? Wha…"

Mom glanced at Granny and Chucky, who were slowly making their way over.

Blinking back tears, I said, "Mom, I am so, so sorry."

Mom stood up and said, "I'm sorry too, baby. I didn't mean any of those horrible things I said."

"Me either," I said, choking back a sob.

Mom wrapped her arms around me. We both just stood there hugging each other, quietly sobbing. I glanced down at Dad's grave. Mom placed her bouquet of flowers on top. Next to the flowers was a Snickers bar.

"You remembered the Snickers."

"Of course. You should have seen the faces of all the people at the gas station when I ran inside in my wedding gown."

I laughed as Mom tightened her embrace. I peeked under her arms at Dad's grave. Since he died so recently, it looked a bit shinier than some of the others. The top of the grave read *Mike O'Connell* and had his date of birth and date of death. Under that was Mom's name and her birthdate. The death date was blank, and hopefully would remain that way for another 60 years. At the bottom of the gravestone was an inscription that read *'Here lies a loving father, husband, son, and uncle who sacrificed himself while defending his country'.*

A bunch of memories suddenly came flooding back. They were memories I hadn't thought about in years.

I remembered how sometimes when my dad would be home on leave, he'd cry out in his sleep. He was normally a very happy guy, but sometimes he'd come back with scars and cuts all over his body, and he would be very sad. I used to ask him what happened; why was he so hurt, why was he so sad, why did he scream in the middle of the night? Dad never wanted to frighten me, so he just said he got into a fight with some bad guys, and he lost a few friends in the process. Now that I was older, I knew exactly what my dad went through. He was a Navy Seal, constantly sent on dangerous missions to the ends of the earth to fight the most evil, real-life super-villains.

I used to think my dad was invincible. I didn't think the bad guys stood a chance against him. He was like a real-life superhero. But he was an even better dad.

Whenever he went overseas, Dad would call and e-mail me to see how I was doing. And when he came home, he'd bring presents and play video games with me, and take me camping and to wrestling matches and all kinds of stuff. He was like my best friend. Everyone loved my dad, but no one loved him more than me.

I remembered the day I lost my dad like it was yesterday. It was the day before spring break. I remembered because I was excited I was going to get a week off of school. Even better, Dad was supposed to come home in a few days.

During the middle of our English lesson, the principal came on over the intercom and called me down to her office. I should have suspected something was wrong from the way her voice cracked, but I was just a little kid. I didn't automatically assume something bad had happened. I mean, it was spring break? What could go wrong?

I would soon find out.

I remember seeing Shawn sitting outside the principal's office. He got in trouble earlier in the day for fighting with Penelope. I walked past him and entered the office.

I was surprised to see my mom and granny standing there with the principal. At first I thought I was in trouble, but then I noticed Mom and Granny had been crying.

Mom rushed over and gave me a smothering hug. I'll never forget her next words.

"Baby, your father isn't coming home."

I completely broke down. Not only did I lose my dad, but I lost my best friend. I spent my entire spring break crying. During the funeral, I totally lost it and had to be taken outside. My whole world had crashed around me. It would take months before I got back to a normal state of mind.

There was one memory that stood out more than all the others. On my first day back from spring break, everyone was super nice to me... my friends, teachers, classmates, the principal, the janitor, the lunch ladies, even Rufus and Cletus...

everyone but Jasper. He started picking on me during recess like he usually did. But it wasn't my friends or a teacher who came to my rescue.

It was Shawn.

Shawn saw Jasper picking on me and told him to stop. Jasper grudgingly walked away. Even back then Shawn had goodness in his heart. It was Jasper who corrupted him.

I don't know how long Mom and I hugged each other, but we broke apart when Chucky and Granny walked over.

"If you guys are truly against this wedding, I guess we can hold off," Mom said sadly.

A sudden breeze sent chills down my spine. It may have been my imagination, but I could have sworn I heard Dad call me from beyond the grave.

*"I'm okay with it, bud. Coach Farmer is a good man. Let your mother be happy again."*

"No, Mom," I said. "Shawn and I were wrong. You deserve to be with who makes you happy, and Coach Farmer is that person. Just because you fell in love with someone else doesn't mean you still don't love Dad."

"Yeah, Ms. O'Connell. Harold and I have been acting stupid," Shawn said, returning from his mother's grave. "Please go back and marry my dad."

Mom's eyes welled up with tears, but this time they were happy ones. She hugged us both. "I love both of you... my sons."

"It will be nice to have a mom again," Shawn said in a cracking voice.

Granny suddenly started bawling and gave us all a crushing bearhug. "This is more precious than anything on my soaps!"

"Okay... Granny.... I... can't... breathe...,"

I gasped.

Granny finally let us go.

Chucky glanced at his cell phone. "If you guys are serious about finishing the wedding, we should head back now. Pastor Max just sent me a text saying people are starting to leave."

Granny pointed her flabby arms in the air and shouted, "To the Granny-mobile!"

"You mean your crummy minivan?" I asked.

"Don't be hating," Granny snapped.

With that, we all rushed over to the cars. Shawn and I rode with my mom. After all, we were about to be one big (sorta) happy family.

Chapter Twenty-One

When we got back to the church, there were still a bunch of people standing out in the parking lot. I noticed a few cars were gone, but it looked like most people decided to stick around.

When Mom got out of the car, everyone broke into applause. Anthony and Jon ran over and hugged her. The aunts hugged her, too. They cried and rambled on about how much they loved their 'sissy'.

Coach Farmer wheeled over and hugged Shawn. "Thanks for bringing Penny back in one piece, bud."

"It's the least I could do, Pops," Shawn said.

Coach looked at me uneasily, like he couldn't decide whether to hug me or holler. He decided to do neither and wheeled over to Mom.

Mom and Coach hugged each other for a long time. When they finally broke apart, Coach said, "If you want to postpone the wedding, babe, I completely understand. I don't want to rush you. I just want you to be happy."

Before Mom could respond, I said, "No, you guys need to get married today."

Mom smiled. Coach Farmer cocked an eyebrow.

"Are you sure?" he asked hesitantly. "I mean, aren't you the one who made our lives miserable these past few weeks?"

"I did have a little help from your son and my mentally unstable granny," I said.

"Hey," Granny said. "I'm not mentally unstable. My psychiatrist even closed his practice and told me to never come back."

"Uhhhh...," was my reply.

I turned back to Coach and held out my hand. "I want you and my mom to get married. I'm willing to try real hard to make this work."

Coach eyed my hand suspiciously. He finally cracked a smile and threw open his arms. "Come here, sport, gimme a hug. Handshakes are for strangers."

I gave Coach a hug, which turned out to be a horrible mistake because he practically suffocated me.

Blubbering like a baby, Coach bawled, "I'm so happy we were able to reconcile, son. I... I love you!"

"I... can't... breathe...," I gasped, wildly flailing my arms.

Thankfully, Mom and Shawn pried us apart.

Pastor Max tapped his watch and said, "Uncle Bob's delicious buffet spread is getting cold, people. Let's finish this wedding so we can eat!"

Everyone murmured about how they were hungry and rushed inside the church. That proved my point that people only came to weddings for the food.

Mom tugged on Pastor Max's sleeve and said, "Just give me a few minutes to freshen up, Max. My mascara is all smeared."

"Sure Penny, we'll start whenever you're ready," Pastor Max said, ushering her inside.

Great Granny gave Granny a hug. I couldn't help but stare. Great Granny never hugged *anyone*.

Granny was clearly shocked. She stepped back and sputtered, "W… what's wrong, Mother? Are you dying?"

"No," Great Granny snapped. "I've still got a good 20, 30 years left. I'm just proud of you for saving Penny's wedding. That *almost* makes up for when you ruined my wedding 20 years ago."

"Oh for crying out loud, Mother, it was two decades ago. Let it go!"

My grannies' brief moment of love was over faster than I could blink. They both went back to bickering as they made their way inside the church.

Soon it was just me and Shawn.

We stood there awkwardly, rocking back and forth on our heels.

Shawn finally said, "Uh, we should probably head in."

"Yeah, I guess," I mumbled. "Hey Shawn?"

Shawn was already at the door. He stopped and turned around. "Huh?"

I wasn't quite sure what I wanted to say. I was having trouble gathering my thoughts. I finally blurted out, "So how are things going to be between us from now on?"

"What do you mean?"

"I think you know exactly what I mean. Our parents are getting married in about two minutes. We're going to be a family. We're going to be *brothers*. Are we going to be cool with each other like we were when this whole mess started, or are we going back to being enemies?"

Shawn looked down. "I… I don't know, Harold. Things are… complicated."

"Why? Because of the Dunces?"

"Well, yeah. I mean, they… I… I don't know."

"You don't need them anymore. You can hang out with me and my friends."

"Oh really? I thought you weren't talking to them since Penelope went behind your back and started dating Ben."

I felt my cheeks flush. I looked down and mumbled, "It's complicated."

"That's what I just said. Look Harold, no offense, but you're the last person on the planet I'd ever go to for advice. You have even more problems than I do."

I shook my head. Things were spiraling out of control again.

And then they got worse.

"Hey losers."

Shawn and I spun around. Jasper, Rufus, and Cletus pulled up on their bikes. I narrowed my eyes when I saw what Jasper was carrying.

A carton of eggs.

"Er, hey guys," Shawn said uneasily. "What are you doing here?"

"We were just in the neighborhood and thought we'd crash the wedding," Jasper sneered. "Did your dad decide to ditch the broad?"

"Wait, did you just call my mom a..."

Shawn held me back. It was a good thing, too, because I was a split-second away from delivering a flying tackle to Jasper's face.

"Actually, the wedding is still on," Shawn said.

"That sucks. Now you have a doofus brother." Jasper pointed at me, I guess in case his cousins got confused. It apparently wasn't enough because Rufus scratched his head and said, "Duh, who's getting married?"

Jasper held up the eggs. "So anyway, me

and my cousins are gonna throw eggs at the senior center. You wanna come, Shawn?"

Granny had just come outside, probably to get me and Shawn for the wedding. She must have overheard Jasper because she hollered, "You hoodlums are the little brats who have been throwing eggs at our center? Wait until I tell the other grannies!"

Granny wobbled back inside the church.

Jasper twirled the egg carton around on his hand. "So what's it gonna be, Shawn? Are you gonna stay here with your lame new brother, or have some fun with us?"

Rufus clapped his hands. "Fun is fun!"

Cletus laughed obnoxiously. They made Blake look like a child prodigy.

An evil smirk suddenly crept across Jasper's evil face.

"Hey, I have an idea. Let's egg O'Connell first, then do the senior center."

"Duh, isn't that kind of mean, Jasper?" Cletus said.

"Duh, yeah," Rufus agreed.

"Yes, you nitwits," Jasper snapped. "That's the point! Now shut up and grab O'Connell."

Before I could move, Cletus and Rufus grabbed my arms.

"Hey, let me go you dunces!" I hollered.

Jasper opened the carton and grabbed a couple eggs. Instead of throwing them at me, though, he handed them to Shawn.

"Why don't you do the honors, Shawn?" Jasper suggested. "Get you some payback for all the hell O'Connell's put you through."

Shawn rolled the eggs around in his hand.

Still squirming, I said, "I can't believe

you're actually thinking about pelting me with eggs. You haven't changed at all, have you?"

Shawn scowled. "How do I know you wouldn't do the same thing to me if our roles were reversed?"

No matter how much I struggled, I couldn't break free from the Dunces' grasp. I finally stopped squirming.

"Go ahead. I don't even care anymore. But if you do this, then our friendship... what little of it there was... is *over*."

Jasper cackled. "How touching. C'mon Shawn, egg him. We ain't got all day."

"You have a choice to make, Shawn," I said in a borderline pleading voice. "Me... or them."

Shawn's face hardened.

"I've already made my choice."

Shawn pulled back his arm. I closed my eyes and waited for gooey eggs to splatter all over my face.

SPLAT!

I heard the eggs explode, but I didn't feel anything. I cracked open my eyes and gasped. Jasper's face was covered in yellow gunk.

Shawn made his choice. He picked *me*.

Jasper wiped his eyes and sputtered, "Shawn... wha... what are you doing?!"

"I'm tired of your bullying ways, Jasper," Shawn replied in a shaky voice. I couldn't blame him for being nervous. He was going head-to-head against the biggest bully in school.

Shawn pointed at Rufus and Cletus. "Let Harold go. *Now*."

Rufus and Cletus immediately released me. I rubbed my throbbing biceps (the Dunces had tight grips) and said, "Thanks, bro."

Shawn smirked. "Don't mention it... bro."

Jasper stomped his foot. "Don't listen to Shawn! I'm the boss! Grab O'Connell and hold him down so I can pound his face in!"

"Duh, okay," Rufus said. He and his brother grabbed me again.

"I told you dunces to let him go," Shawn snapped

The Dunces released me.

"What are you doing?" Jasper exploded. "Grab him!"

Rufus started to cry. "I'm so confused."

"Hold me, brother," Cletus wailed.

Rufus and Cletus cried into each other's arms. It was actually kind of disturbing to watch.

"Oh for crying out loud," Jasper growled. "If you want something done right, you gotta do it yourself."

Jasper started to march toward me, but Shawn jumped in the way.

"Leave him alone, dude. Just go away."

"No." Jasper shoved Shawn in the chest, knocking him flat on his butt. He then picked up his carton of eggs.

"I think I'm gonna make me an omelet... on your face."

Jasper opened the carton. Before he could turn it upside down on top of Shawn, I rushed over and smacked his arm. The carton flipped over and a dozen eggs splattered all over his head. Shawn burst out laughing. Rufus and Cletus laughed, too.

Jasper quivered in rage. "I'm gonna beat the crud out of both of you."

Jasper grabbed me by my tie and pulled back his fist. I shut my eyes and hoped I didn't lose all my teeth.

"There they are, girls!"

I opened my eyes. My grannies had just wobbled outside with a dozen of their granny friends. And they were all holding eggs. I guess they stole them from Uncle Bob.

"Who are we egging again?" Great Granny asked, squinting at us through her bifocals.

"The fat, ugly, bald children," Granny replied. "They're the ones who have been throwing eggs at our precious senior center."

An enormous, gray-haired granny wobbled toward us and bellowed, "Jasper, put that boy down!"

Jasper immediately let me go.

"G…G…Grandma Dunce?" Jasper sputtered. He sounded absolutely petrified.

"That demon child is your grandson, Edna?" Granny asked.

"Unfortunately," grumbled Grandma Dunce. "He's a rotten brat, just like his father. So Jasper, you and your dingbat cousins have been desecrating our senior center?"

Jasper stuttered, "N… no, Grandma. We'd never do nothing like that!"

I covered my mouth to stifle my chuckles. Jasper's grandma was even meaner than Great Granny. Jasper was scared to death of her. She'd make one heck of a detention monitor.

Rocket scientist Rufus ruined Jasper's cover by saying, "Duh, what are you talking about, Jasper? We always egg the senior center."

"Duh, yeah," chimed in brain surgeon Cletus. "In fact, we was just about to go there now."

Grandma Dunce flipped open her carton of eggs. "Fire at will, ladies!"

"Get outta the way, Harold!" Granny hollered.

Shawn and I dashed behind my grannies.

"Run for it, boys!" Jasper hollered, hopping on his bike

Rufus and Cletus ran around like chickens with their heads cut off. They collided into one another and fell down.

Granny, Great Granny, Grandma Dunce, and all their blue-haired friends fired off a volley of eggs. Jasper hadn't even gone ten feet before several of the eggs exploded against his backside. Rufus and Cletus got splattered as they clambered to their feet and hopped on their bikes. They both cried as they rode off down the street, eggs drenching them from head to toe.

My grannies and their pals cheered.

"That'll show them no-good, doo-doo headed brats," Granny chuckled.

"After the wedding, let's go egg their school," Great Granny suggested.

"Oh, can I join?" Coach Bebop asked, sticking her head out the front door. "I hate that place."

My grannies and their pals wobbled back inside the church. Shawn grinned and patted me on the back as we followed them. No words even needed to be said. My new brother stuck up for me when it mattered most. Things would be different between us from there on out... for the better.

Chapter Twenty-Two

We all gathered back in the auditorium area of the church. I sat with Shawn and my grannies. Quite a few people had already left, so we had a bit more breathing room. I was happy to see all my friends were still there, though. I'd have to make amends with them at the reception.

Since everyone was starving and irritable, Pastor Max jumped right into the good stuff. He had Mom and Coach Farmer exchange their vows, then said, "Before I make this blessed union official in the eyes of God, is there anyone who thinks these two should not wed? If so, speak now or forever..."

Mom shouted, "Nope, let's skip that part. That's what held us up last time."

Everyone laughed. Even I found it pretty funny.

Pastor Max smiled. "Good idea. I now pronounce you husband and wife. You may now kiss the bride."

Mom surprised everyone by grabbing Coach Farmer's face and giving him a big, wet, sloppy kiss on the lips. Everyone cheered (except for Coach Bebop, who looked like she was about to puke).

Granny jumped up and thrust her fist in the air. "Thata-girl! Use that tongue!"

Great Granny hobbled to her feet and shouted, "Get a room, whippersnappers!"

Coach Heffer started bawling and blew his nose on his tie. "Weddings always make me cry!" he wailed.

Carl and Roger did their best to console Coach Heffer.

With the wedding officially over, it was time to party. Usually the groom carried the bride down the aisle, but since Coach Farmer was in a wheelchair, Mom sat on his lap and he wheeled them over to the reception area. Everyone followed after them.

When I walked into the reception room, I gasped and nearly fainted. Uncle Bob had set out six giant buffet tables overflowing with every food imaginable. It was even better than his restaurant!

"Hummina hummina hummina," Granny said, slobbering all over her double chin. She shoved everyone out of the way so she was first in line.

Shawn and I got a heaping plate of food and chatted with Chucky and his band mates, Diamond, Buster, and Blade. Abdul and Blake eventually wandered over. I told them I was sorry for acting like a jerk the past few weeks and asked if there were any hard feelings. Abdul said no. Blake said glue tasted better than paint. I simply nodded and said I could see that being the case.

As we were chatting, I noticed Penelope out of the corner of my eye. I turned and watched as she made a plate of food. Ben was behind her. His mouth was flapping like a duck's behind. Penelope looked a tad annoyed. I found that funny.

Shawn nudged me. "You should go talk to her, dude."

I felt my face turn red. "She probably doesn't want anything to do with me," I grumbled.

"Not after the way I've acted."

"I don't know, man," Abdul said, tearing into a chicken leg. "She's been awfully upset ever since you guys started fighting."

"Really?" I asked.

"Yep. I think Ben is really getting on her nerves. He annoys us when we only hang out with him for a few hours. Can you imagine being around him all the time?"

I shivered at the thought.

Jon and Anthony suddenly ran past Ben, squirting water guns. Ben exclaimed, "I wanna join!" and ran after them.

"Look man, she's all alone," Shawn said, nudging me again. "Go!"

"Alright, alright." I slowly made my way toward Penelope. Halfway there I turned around. Shawn, Abdul, Blake, Chucky, and Chucky's pals were staring at me with huge grins.

"Go!" Shawn said, flapping his arms.

"Alright!" I hollered. I turned around and walked right up to Penelope.

Penelope was facing the wall, eating some mac and cheese. I cleared my throat to get her attention.

Penelope sighed. "Look Ben, I told you to leave me alone for a little while. You're really starting to annoy…"

Penelope turned around. Her anger and irritation faded away to shock and embarrassment.

"Oh. Uh, hi Harold."

"Hi," I said sheepishly.

"So how have you been?" Penelope asked awkwardly.

"Good. And you?" I asked, just as awkwardly.

"Good."

We both stood there and didn't say another word for at least ten seconds. It was like we were walking on egg shells. I couldn't believe that we were having trouble striking up a conversation. Just a week ago, we would have been talking for hours on end about all sorts of stuff, but now we couldn't even think of anything beyond, *"Hi, how are you?"* Things had gotten out of hand. I needed to fix our friendship before it slipped away forever.

"I'm really glad you came," I stammered.

Penelope smiled faintly. "My parents kinda forced me to, but you know I love your mom."

"And I like your dress. It's very... pretty," I said, not quite sure if I should use the word *pretty* around Penelope. Normally she'd punch me if I said she looked nice. She was such a tomboy.

Penelope blushed. "Oh, uh, thanks! I don't normally wear dresses, as you know, but I figured I should dress nice for your mom's big day. You look nice, too."

Now I was blushing. "Thanks."

"Ben said I look silly in a dress," Penelope said. Her voice had a hint of bitterness to it.

"Ben's an idiot," I replied.

Penelope grinned again.

We were quiet for another ten seconds. I finally decided to throw all caution to the wind.

Talking 100 miles-an-hour, I said, "Look Penelope, I'm sorry I've been such a jerk to you. The truth is, I really like you. Like *like you* like you. When I found out you were dating Ben, I got super jealous. Really it's all my fault. Instead of pretending to like cheesy pop singers and dressing like a vampire just so I could impress April Summers, I should have been myself and hung out with you. You're like my best friend and I don't want to lose you."

I took a deep breath. I was afraid I talked so fast that Penelope hadn't heard me. I was even more afraid she had heard me and now thought I was an idiot.

Penelope grinned. "Wait. You... you like me?"

I looked down at my shoes. "Yeah," I mumbled. "You're the coolest girl I know. You like wrestling, video games, comic books... you're an amazing athlete, you're pretty, and... well, I like girls who can beat me up."

"You think I'm pretty?"

I looked up. Penelope's eyes were slightly moist, like she was on the verge of spilling a few tears. It suddenly occurred to me no one had ever told Penelope she was pretty before. It was probably because guys were afraid she'd tear their heads off.

"Yeah. You're very pretty."

Penelope was about to say something, but Ben rushed over and slapped me on the back.

"What's up, Fatman? Long time no talk," he said with a cheesy grin. His hair was dripping wet, I guess from his water gun fight with Jon and Anthony. "So what were you guys talking about?"

"Nothing, Ben," Penelope snapped. I could tell she was mad he interrupted us. "Why don't you go back and play with the kids?"

"Nah, I'm good. C'mon, they're about to cut the cake. Let's get close so we can get a piece. I know how much you like to eat."

Ben grabbed Penelope's hand. Penelope yanked it back.

Ben cocked an eyebrow. "What's wrong?" He turned to me and narrowed his eyes. "Oh, wait, I know what's going on. Fatman's trying to steal you from me, huh? He couldn't hack it with April Summers, so now he's trying to take my girl."

"She's not *your* girl," I said angrily. "What do you think this is, the 1800s?"

"Thank you, Harold," Penelope said.

Ben shoved me in the chest. "Butt out, Fatman. This has nothing to do with you. Why don't you go hang out with Oinky? You two were made for each other. You're both fat."

Ben laughed obnoxiously. I couldn't take it anymore. I was tired of being made fun of. I wasn't going to take it from the Dunces, and I definitely wasn't going to take it from my so-called friend.

"Quit calling me Fatman!" I exploded. "I'm big-boned!"

I shoved Ben so hard that he fell flat on his back. He looked up at me and started to cry.

"Ouch! That hurt! I'm telling your granny!"

Ben jumped up and ran over to Granny. He was too far away for me to hear what he was saying, but I could tell from the way he wildly flailed his arms that he was ratting me out. Granny looked over at me and keeled over in laughter. Ben started crying again and ran into the bathroom.

I turned back to Penelope and mumbled, "Sorry. I didn't mean to knock over your boyfriend."

Penelope smirked. "Please, you did me a favor. I was going to dump him anyway. He's so annoying."

"Do you think he won't want to be friends with us anymore?"

Penelope shrugged. "He probably won't talk to us for a few days, but he'll come crawling back. Who else will put up with him?"

I laughed and grabbed Penelope's hand. "C'mon. Let's get some cake."

Penelope and I joined the rest of the wedding guests and gathered around Mom and Coach Farmer, who were standing before a giant, white-iced wedding cake. It was the most beautiful thing I'd ever seen. I would have eaten the entire thing if Mom let me!

Coach Farmer cut two pieces and handed one to Mom. Mom picked it up and acted like she was about to take a bite, but then she shoved it into Coach Farmer's face. Everyone burst out laughing and clapped. Coach picked up his piece and shoved it in Mom's face. Everyone laughed (except for Great Granny, who said they shouldn't waste food).

Little Anthony suddenly ran over and shoved his tiny fist into the bottom of the cake. Before anyone could stop him, he pulled his fist out and tossed a chunk of the cake at Great Granny's head. Great Granny screamed bloody murder and chased Anthony all over the church. Everyone cracked up. Grandma Dunce laughed so hard that she had to be escorted outside for some air.

"That alone was worth me wearing a dress," Penelope said with a grin.

We all got a piece of cake and chowed down. Granny grabbed a microphone and shouted, "Can I have everyone's attention please?"

All the chatter died down. Granny wobbled over to Uncle Bob and Oinky and said, "I have an announcement. Uncle Bob and I have been secretly dating for the past two weeks, and we've fallen madly in love. That's why we've decided to get married."

Uncle Bob spit out his cake. "Wait, what? I thought we were just talking about it!"

Granny flapped her wrist. "Same difference. Anyway, we're getting married!"

There were scattered rounds of applause. But mostly people were just shocked, including my entire family. Poor Oinky about had a nervous breakdown. He ran back and forth, leaving little presents all over the place.

"I need some chocolate," Mom said, hurrying over to the buffet table.

Shortly after Granny's stunning news, Chucky and his band mates played some more punk rock. A bunch of people went to the middle of the reception area and danced. Even Granny and her granny friends busted a move.

I turned to Penelope and nervously said, "So did you want to… um… you know, would you like to… uh…"

Penelope cracked a smile. "Are you trying to ask me if I'd like to dance?"

"Yeah," I said, feeling like a total moron.

"I'd love to." Penelope grabbed my hands and dragged me out to the dance floor.

"Now make sure you don't step on my feet," Penelope said seriously.

We only danced for ten seconds before I did exactly that. But it was all good because Penelope stomped on my foot in retaliation.

In the middle of a raunchy song that Chucky never would have been allowed to sing at school (and Pastor Max didn't look too thrilled to have played in his church), I glanced around at all my friends and family. Mom was dancing with Coach Farmer, swinging him around the dance floor in his wheelchair. Jon and Anthony were still chasing each other, shooting water guns. Great Granny and her senior pals were doing the hokey pokey and some dance moves they learned during the Great Depression. Granny and Uncle Bob were doing the cabbage patch dance. Roger and Carl were hitting on the aunts, who kept giggling like little school girls. (Guys normally didn't pay a lot of attention to them.) Shawn was flirting with this older, hot girl my mom worked with. (I'm pretty sure she was in college, but he didn't let that faze him.) Blake and Abdul were dancing with Grandma Dunce. Ben finally came out of the bathroom and chased after Jon and Anthony. Coach Heffer continued to stand off in the corner, bawling. Coach Bebop rolled her eyes and patted him on the back, offering emotional support. And Paul Diamond and Sarah Lung were doing the Monster Mash. (Don't ask.)

As Penelope smacked me for stepping on her foot again, I thought about how after everything that happened, not much had changed. My family and friends were still as wacky and annoying as ever. But now I realized how lucky I was to have them.

Mom's wedding to Coach Farmer turned out to be one of the best days of my life. The school bully had been transformed. He was now my brother... and my *friend*.

Made in United States
North Haven, CT
17 June 2023

37877472R00117